CUPID CRAZY

RETURN TO CUPID, TEXAS #10

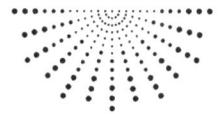

SYLVIA MCDANIEL

Want to learn about my new releases before anyone else? Sign up for my New Book Alert on www.SylviaMcDaniel.com and receive a free book.

Childhood enemies married in Vegas?

Caitlyn Beckett, had a five year plan. Marry a handsome billionaire, have two point five children and live happily-ever-after in a grand mansion. Only problem, she is four years late in finding her wealthy husband and is beginning to feel desperate.

Nathan Greene and Caitlyn have hated each other since Junior high when they ran against each other for the Student Council President and his slogan was the Brains to Get it Done. Since that day she's made her feelings for him quite clear. Now he's desperate to find a wife and with them both attending her sister's Vegas wedding, she's the perfect target. For ninety days, he needs a marriage of convenience.

Can the two of them live under the same roof without killing each other?

CHAPTER ONE

*D*etermined to marry a rich man, Caitlyn Beckett had a problem. Her sister Whitney was marrying the only billionaire in her small town. Somehow, she needed to search outside the boundaries of Cupid, Texas to find a wealthy man.

The travel brochures in her purse were one of her tools to help her reach that goal.

She was going to fly to St. Tropez–the playground of the extraordinarily rich–meet a billionaire, and marry him.

Her only problem?

She needed at least thirty thousand dollars for her luxury vacation in order to find a well-to-do husband. At this time, she was about twenty-seven thousand dollars short.

A cheer brought her back to the bachelorette party she and her sister, Heather, were hosting at the Cupid Hotel for their other sister, Whitney.

As Caitlyn Beckett watched the bride-to-be dance with her friends, she knew her sister had never been happier. Although Whitney was marrying a man Caitlyn had once wanted for herself, she felt no ill-will and was genuinely excited for her sister. The couple were perfect for one another, and Caitlyn felt she deserved every bit of the happiness was showing.

Whitney had requested a low-key party, but Caitlyn and Heather had rented a room, along with a DJ to play music. The bridal party were spending the night at the hotel, so they could celebrate all night long.

Close to midnight all their friends left, and it was just the smaller group now. The wedding would take place a week from that very day. By this time next week, Caitlyn's sister would be someone's wife.

During the DJ's break, the women all sank down at the tables to rest.

"Tell us how you met Aaron," one of the girls called out.

Whitney smiled, and Caitlyn laughed as her sister began to tell her story.

"He was the best-friend of my ex-fiancé and I hadn't seen him for years, until the night I picked him up running naked down the street. Max Vandenburg convinced him to do the Cupid Stupid Dance, and I was the one who stopped to pick him up."

Long ago, Caitlyn would have done the dance herself, *if* she believed in that nonsense, and *if* the statue could guarantee a rich husband.

But how many wealthy men—other than Aaron—would do the Cupid Stupid Dance?

Aaron was the only one she knew who'd taken the chance on finding love and had done the dance.

The superstition had been handed down through the generations, with everyone agreeing to the same details. It's said the first person you see after you run naked around the statue at midnight, would be your one true love.

Caitlyn didn't believe in it one bit. However, if they had a statue with the same superstition attached to it in St Tropez, France, she'd run naked around it in a heartbeat.

Sarah sighed. "How romantic."

"I want to get married," Lauren, Whitney's friend, said. "Let's go do the Cupid Stupid Dance!"

"No," Heather said firmly. "I'm not risking everything on the off chance I might find love."

Caitlyn couldn't blame her for saying no. Her sister had been studying so hard for the bar exam the following month, and it would be devastating for her to lose it all over one night of meaningless fun.

"What about you, Caitlyn?"

Why would *she* do something so ridiculous, especially when she already knew what she wanted wasn't available in this small town?

"My sister is marrying the only rich man in Cupid. No thanks. I'll pass and wait for a guaranteed billionaire."

"Let's do it," Michelle said, struggling to her feet, her legs wobbly from a bit too much alcohol. "Tonight, one week from Valentine's Day. A week before Whitney's dream wedding in Vegas, I'm going to take a chance on love. Who's with me?"

Sarah squeaked. "I am!"

Lauren jumped to her feet and turned to Caitlyn. "Oh come on! You're always talking about how you want to find a husband. Or is that all it is…just talk?"

"No, I plan on getting married the moment I find a wealthy man to entice. So why would I waste my time on any man here in Cupid?"

Amanda, her arch enemy, the one girl in town who had never forgiven Caitlyn for being more popular than her in high school, stood and glared at her. Why her sister invited her she didn't know. "If you don't believe the superstition is real, then you shouldn't be worried about who you'll see after you dance naked around the statue. Caitlyn is afraid of getting caught is all. She's chicken. But you can count me in!"

Amanda's ploy was easy to recognize, but Caitlyn could never overlook a taunt. Everyone who had ever had their hair cut at her beauty salon, Beauty and Brains, knew she would not settle for a man whose bank account had less than eight figures.

"All right, I'll do the Cupid Stupid Dance with you, but I'm not afraid of who I will meet because I'm certain of my destiny. I'm marrying a rich man in St. Tropez."

They all laughed, but this was her fate, and there would be no denying her.

"How do you plan on getting there?" Amanda asked.

"By flying of course," she said, knowing it would take a lot more cash than she had at the moment. Whitney shook her head at them all. "Heather and I will be waiting in the car to pick you up. Don't spoil tonight by me having to bail you out of jail. We're all flying to Vegas in less than a week."

After Whitney's first disastrous attempt at getting married in Cupid, she'd decided, *this* time, she would have a destination wedding. So on Thursday, friends and family would all fly to Vegas, and the ceremony would be Saturday evening.

Michelle stood. "We've got fifteen minutes before it hits midnight. If we're doing this, let's get a move on."

What in the hell had Caitlyn just agreed to do?

It was late; who would be out this time of night?

Likely no one.

So what would it hurt?

She would do the dance and avoid meeting anyone, because *no one* would be there to spoil her plans of marrying a rich man.

That is, *if* the superstition were true…which it's not.

CHAPTER TWO

*I*mmediately after the funeral for his uncle, Nathan Greene decided to drive home to Cupid, Texas. It was late, he was tired, and frankly, he wanted to escape his extended family. The vultures had begun circling around the old man's corpse, just waiting to see who would inherit the deceased bachelor's millions.

He didn't stick around to find out who all got what. Even in death, Uncle John didn't deserve to be treated with such disrespect. So he left before his kinfolk began turning on each other.

Nathan didn't have time for that nonsense. Not only did he work his butt off for Aaron Johnson, but he also had a side hustle teaching young men how to be a professional gamer, along with an app he'd created, which gave away moves to advance you to the next level in the most popular games.

His business was flourishing, and if it wasn't for his uncle's funeral, and Aaron's wedding he still had to prepare for the following weekend, he would be at home working, training, and doing everything possible to make his first million.

Two blocks from home, he turned down Main Street and was shocked when, suddenly, four naked women came screaming out of the park, scattering off in different directions, with the sheriff running from the park behind them.

The sight was shocking indeed, yet comical as well.

Laughing, he shook his head. Everyone living in Cupid, Texas, knew of the superstition, but this was the first time Nathan had ever witnessed anyone actually running from the law after performing the ritual.

And doing so naked as the day they were born, no less!

Whoa! Wait a minute.

Was that…?

Is that…?

Caitlyn?

Caitlyn Beckett swerved away from the women and darted out in front of his car. He slammed on the brakes to keep from hitting her.

As much as he tried not to like the woman, he couldn't help feeling attracted to her.

Yet, she'd never forgiven him for making fun of her when they'd both run for student council clear back in junior high. One of those young, male macho times, where he longed to appear big for the guys, and in doing so, lost her friendship. Stupid on his part, and all just to satisfy his immature ego.

His Mustang came to a halt in the middle of the street, his headlights shining on her naked body. He rolled down the window, unable to take his eyes off her. The woman was even more beautiful than his nerdy brain had ever imagined.

"Hop in the car!" Nathan shouted, knowing the sheriff could arrive any second.

Why they decided tonight would be the ideal time to do the Cupid Dance, he didn't know. From now until after Valentine's Day, the law would be watching for the Cupid Stupid dancers.

The look Caitlyn sent him should have caused him to gun the gas and hurtle the car down the street. But he'd always had a soft spot for the woman who had never forgiven him for creating such an uproar in junior high.

She glared at him. "You really know how to screw things up!"

What had he done, besides try to rescue her?

"Do you want a ride, or would you rather be arrested?" he asked, irritated she was resisting his attempt to save her.

"I would stand nude on the corner of Main Street, in broad daylight, before I accept a ride with *you*," she said. "Beauty and Brains."

She taunted the familiar old slogan she'd used to beat him with when they'd both run for class president. The words still caused a sizzle to race up his spine.

"You're proving my point; Brains would get in the car," he retorted. "Enjoy jail; I'm sure you'll be treated like the princess you *think* you are."

Always considered a nerd, he had stepped out of his comfort zone all those years ago and had made his campaign slogan, the words of which only someone much more confident in himself than he actually was would have done. It was: *The brains needed to get the job done*—insinuating *he* was the one with the brains.

But she had counter-responded with: *Beauty* and *brains: A winning combination.*

And she'd won, regardless of the fact every gamer in school had campaigned for *him*.

Pressing the Mustang's gas pedal, he shot down the street, leaving her standing alone. A sense of guilt gripped him, but he couldn't force her into the vehicle, even if it *was* for her own good.

Instead, he drove around the block, hoping to distract the sheriff.

When was she ever going to forgive him for a stupid campaign which pitted girls against boys, and was so long ago? Hell! They were just kids really.

Of course, calling her a princess this evening probably hadn't helped.

But, *damn*, the woman was gorgeous; in a sweet and inno-cent–and *frustrating!*–kind of way.

All these years later, whatever blind crazy feelings he still had for her, he knew he needed to cauterize. It was long past time to put his feelings for Caitlyn behind him.

And yet…he knew it would likely never happen.

Groaning, he turned the Mustang around, not wanting her to go to jail.

But when he drove back down the road to the place he'd last seen her, she was nowhere to be found.

Had the sheriff found and arrested her?

CHAPTER THREE

"Where the hell have you been?" Caitlyn admonished her sister, Heather, as she jumped into the car, her bare cheeks squeaking on the leather as they slid across the seat.

Not only was the temperature falling below freezing, but the sheriff was still searching for them. She'd been hiding behind a garbage bin, wondering why the hell she'd allowed someone she didn't even give a damn about to taunt her into doing something so stupid.

She was too old for this crap!

"Where do you think? Looking for you."

With a toss of her blonde curls, Caitlyn grabbed her clothes from the back and started dressing as her sister drove down the street towards the park.

The sooner she was dressed, the safer she would feel.

"Where are you going?" Caitlyn asked, knowing the law roamed the streets, hunting for the naked women. "The sheriff chased us out of the park."

Heather whirled to face her. "Did he catch anyone?"

"I don't know. I ran in the opposite direction from everyone else, and he went after the other three."

"Let's hope we don't need to bail a bridesmaid out of jail tonight," Heather said, gazing up in her rear-view mirror. "Hurry up and get the rest of your clothes on in case we get pulled over."

They drove through the trees slowly while keeping an eye out for the naked girls. The statue could not be seen from the road, and Caitlyn was not about to jump out of the car and go in search of the other women.

"They're not here," Heather said. "Let's head back to the hotel; maybe Whitney picked them up."

That had been too close a call. A foolish one on her part, especially after she'd run into Nathan Greene.

"So did you see anyone?"

A growling noise erupted from Caitlyn as the car barreled down Main Street.

"Who is the one guy I would *never* in a *million* years marry? Who has also been my arch enemy *ever since junior high*?"

The man she secretly considered to be incredibly attractive, but would admit to no one, not even her sisters.

Heather began to laugh so hard, Caitlyn worried about their safety with her hysterical sister behind the wheel.

"Yes, you must be thinking of the same man I am, and this just proves this is a bogus, superstition that will never work. The man stopped and offered to give me a ride. Like I'm going to crawl naked into his car."

Turning the corner, Heather drove them towards the hotel, tears streaming down her cheeks as she giggled. "Wow, I'm glad I didn't do the Cupid Stupid Dance. When are you ever going to learn not to react to people's taunts? All anyone has to do is dare you, and you'll do just about anything."

As much as she hated hearing the words, her sister was right. Another not too bright decision she's made.

"Are you going to tell the bridesmaids you ran into Nathan? According to legend, he's your man."

Part of Caitlyn wanted to tell everyone because she believed this would, once and for all, prove the Cupid Stupid Dance was fake. If she told the bachelorette party, the girls would assume they were going to marry and would try to link them together. Plus, the news would spread across town like a wildfire.

Oh, no, it would be better if she lied. If anyone asked, the only person she found tonight was Heather, who rescued her from the sheriff.

"No, and you are sworn to secrecy. Please don't tell a soul. Everyone will assume this is a match made in heaven, and frankly, Mr. Brainiac Nerd probably doesn't have enough cash to keep himself in game controllers."

"What if he tells the whole town he saw you naked? What if he tells the town he was the first person you ran into after doing the Cupid Dance?"

Why did her logical, intelligent sister have to think of all the angles?

Already she could hear him telling that group of men children he hung with that he'd seen her curves. They would think they were a couple. That she would choose a man more interested in gaming than a woman. Oh, no. Hell no.

"I'll deny I saw him and say he's such a pathetic little man. Still trying to outsmart me for beating him back in Junior High." Not only had she beat him becoming the student council president, she destroyed him and all his nerdy friends at the local Tomb Raider championship. "Everyone in town knows we're not friends."

Heather stared at her. "Of all the people for you to run into tonight. Too bad. I was hoping you would meet someone you would fall in love with."

"In this small town? Our sister is marrying the only eligible male I would consider."

No, she didn't believe in the superstition, and wasn't disappointed at all. Someday soon, she would meet her husband on a tropical island with wealthy men on every corner. Thirty thousand dollars for her dream vacation to find and marry her rich husband. All part of her five-year plan.

"Nathan and I will never be compatible. Never," she said with force.

Funny how, until junior high, she'd had a crush on him. But since he and his geeky friends jeered at her, they were like an oxygen tent and a cigarette. Instant explosion.

Only she came out the winner, taking home the trophy.

Zipping up her pants, she gazed at the hotel, ready for her sister's bachelorette party to end. Tonight could have been disastrous. As it was, her arch enemy had seen her naked.

Why had she allowed herself to be talked into doing the Cupid Stupid Dance?

"You better hope he keeps his lips shut. Since you two dislike each other so much, I'm not betting he will remain quiet."

No, meeting someone here in Cupid was not part of the plan. The plan needed for her to keep her head down, continue working and saving towards her goal of finding her Mr. Perfect. And no, Nathan Greene would *never* be her Mr. Perfect.

She reached over and touched her sister on the arm. "This is our secret. You can't tell anyone who I ran into on Main Street. And if Nathan says anything, you'll say he's a liar."

Caitlyn knew Heather well enough to know that last bit was a stretch. Truth was everything to her law-abiding sister.

"I'll keep this our secret, but I won't lie," Heather said, as she opened the car door. "Now let's go find the others and see how they fared. Surely someone met her Prince Charming tonight."

CHAPTER FOUR

$\mathcal{T}$wo days before he left for Las Vegas for his best friend's wedding, Nathan sat going over the figures from his online app. The gaming app he'd created, which gave away clues on how to make it to the next level on numerous different games, was doing quite well.

Along with the work he did for his friend, Aaron, this year, he had the potential to make almost a million dollars. Most of that money he'd invested in stocks, and soon he would be investing even more in real estate. Not bad for a twenty-seven-year-old single man.

The image of Caitlyn running, holding her breasts as she sprinted naked down Main Street, came to mind. Years ago, he'd had a crush on her in junior high, which was quickly dashed when she'd turned his slogan on him and crushed him with the whole beauty and brains crap.

The final blow to his heart was when she'd beaten him in the finals of the tournament for playing the game *Tomb Raider*.

Girls weren't supposed to like gaming, and should never crush him at his game. *Never.*

And yet, Caitlyn had not only won–and crushed him thoroughly–but had also taken home the grand prize.

Even today that memory stung. Did she still game?

Win tournaments?

The doorbell rang, and he rose from his computer and went to the door.

A man from FedEx stood there. Opening the door, the man said, "Signature please."

With a frown, Nathan signed for the package, wondering who had sent him something overnight.

After he handed the scanner back to the driver, the man smiled at him and handed him the envelope.

"Thanks."

Nathan turned to go back into the house, but stopped when he glanced down at the return address, and frowned.

Why would a lawyer be sending him anything?

Tearing open the envelope, he pulled out the paperwork, along with a letter from his uncle's lawyer. Quickly, he scanned the letter, his heart pounding in his chest.

An envelope was paperclipped to the lawyer's letter, and he recognized his uncle's handwriting. With a rip, he opened the envelope and stared at the letter from his uncle.

Dearest Nathan,

If you're reading this letter, then I must have departed this world. I'm sure the family has circled around my last will and testament and are eager to start dividing my wealth.

Over the years, I've watched you grow up, and I've seen myself, a hard worker, in you. The only problem is, I let my work become my entire world, just like I see you doing.

It was always my intention to marry a woman later, after I made my first million. Then my second and even my third. By the time I got to my fourth million, I had waited too late.

Because I believe you're making the same mistakes I made, I'm leaving you my money with some stipulations. When you receive this letter, if you are not already married, I'm giving you ninety days to find a wife.

You must remain married for at least ninety-one days. Forever would be better, but I can't control everything in your life. If you do not marry, everyone in the family receives ten thousand dollars, and the balance of the money will go to charity.

Family is everything. Don't wait too late, like I did. Find a woman, fall in love, marry, and have children. Work hard, but not so hard you lose sight of what's important: Family.

Spend this cash wisely, young man. I'll be watching from above, so don't make me regret my decision.

Live your life to the fullest.

John Greene

He glanced at the documents in the folder showing his uncle's wealth and staggered into a chair. As if in a dream, he stared at the figures and realized, if this was true, he was truly close to becoming a billionaire.

But he had no wife. And there was no one he would consider marrying.

The memory of a blonde racing down Main Street, her long limbs and sassy tempting mouth a beacon he suddenly longed for. According to the superstition, he was the man for her.

Could he somehow convince her to marry him?

Maybe in Vegas?

They were both attending her sister's wedding this weekend.

Could he *bribe* her into marrying him?

The woman hated him.

Startled, he jumped up and ran into his office. At the keyboard, he started to search how to get married in Vegas.

With a smile, he stared at the information.

Was it as simple as it sounded?

The courthouse stayed open until midnight.

After her sister's wedding, could he somehow court and convince her to do a quickie ceremony in Vegas?

Would she stay with him for at least ninety-one days before she ended their farce of a marriage? Just long enough for him to gain control of his Uncle's money.

Shaking his head, he wondered if he was crazy. *Cupid* Crazy.

CHAPTER FIVE

*C*aitlyn stared at the crowded room and watched as Whitney and Aaron danced their first dance together as man and wife. She looked so beautiful, but the moment was bittersweet. Sure, Caitlyn was extremely happy for Whitney and Aaron, but this would change everything.

The three sisters were close and now the first one had married. Soon, there would be children and babies and–

With a sigh, she took another sip of champagne and wiped away a tear.

Everyone cheered the newlyweds, as Heather walked up beside Caitlyn.

"They're a beautiful couple. Do you still wish he would have dated you?"

"Hell no," Caitlyn said. "He's not my billionaire. He's Whitney's. Mine is still waiting on me to arrive in St. Tropez."

Heather laughed. "And just how are you going to get to St. Tropez?"

"I'm working on it. A dream vacation, a cute meet on the beach, coming home with my husband in tow..."

In her mind, the scene was set: a love story on a tropical

island. The two of them bumping into each other, laughing, going out to dinner, and the relationship of her and Mr. Perfect growing and expanding, until he finally asked her to marry him.

"Well, don't ask Daddy for any money. He's mad at Mother for spending so much on Whitney's wedding."

Aaron had paid for everything but the reception and her dress, including everyone's rooms. What did her father have to complain about? As the town mayor, her father was the biggest tightwad in Cupid, Texas, and would never help her with funds to St. Tropez. "Don't worry, I knew better than to ask."

They watched as their father took Whitney in his arms to dance. "I'm surprised she's still talking to him."

"Oh, I think after Aaron made that huge donation to the Library, all has been forgiven," Heather said. "Did you see that Nathan is over on the side observing everything and everyone? He keeps glancing your way."

She gazed in his direction and he raised his glass of champagne to her. A tremor raced down her spine.

Why in the world was she attracted to him?

Part of her wanted to flip him off, but instead she gave him a smirky smile and lifted her glass.

The man could take his gaming buddies and go straight to hell.

"And he's your Cupid Love," Heather said laughing.

"Shut up, Heather," she hissed. "No one is supposed to know."

"You better hope and pray that the Cupid Superstition is not true," she said.

One of the bridesmaids walked up to Heather and whispered in her ear. Together the two of them strolled away, leaving Caitlyn standing at the table, alone, watching her sister's reception. With a sigh, she turned to walk away when a hand touched her elbow.

"You look even more stunning with your clothes on," he said.

His voice sent a spiral of heat racing through her.

What was it about this man which seemed to always cause her body to take notice of him?

And why was he being friendly to her?

"I think that's the first nice thing you've said to me since junior high. Are you ill?"

"No, I think it's time we buried the hatchet. We were in junior high when this happened."

"Funny, you're now doing this after you saw me naked. Is this a coincidence?"

He laughed. "Hey, I like your curves, but no, your sister married my best friend. We're going to be at parties, baby showers, children's birthdays and everything else being friends entails, so we need to put the past behind us."

She frowned at him, then realized what he was saying was true. As much as she didn't like him, they would be thrown together all the time.

"Kids will never understand why we keep sparring with one another."

Children. Aaron and her sister would someday have babies, and she couldn't wait to hold and squeeze and spoil them. She was determined she would be their favorite aunt. The man was right, those children would not understand their constant bickering.

"Okay, we're going to bury the hatchet, so to speak. How do we go from enemies to friends?"

Their relationship had always been so tumultuous, it would be hard to switch her thinking from disdainful enemy to reluctant acceptance.

He grinned at her in a way which made her smile. "Dance with me."

Stunned, she stood staring at him. "What?"

"Music is playing. Dance with me and then let me buy you a drink," he said taking her by the elbow and gently leading her towards the floor where people were gyrating to the music.

The touch of his hands on her felt good, but she didn't want to be attracted to him. He was not her Prince Charming, and she had a five-year plan to meet and marry the man of her dreams.

She let him lead her out into the crowd, and she moved into his embrace. "Everyone is staring."

"That's because they're shocked you're in my arms."

"As well they should be. How long has this feud existed?"

"Fourteen years, and it comes to an end today."

"Or we could make them think we've made up, then start something all over again."

"I knew you were going to be trouble," he said with a grin.

"Keeps life from being boring–and *hey*!–we do have lots of animosity between us."

"Not anymore. Now smile," he said.

"Wow, you're serious," she said, wondering why suddenly he seemed so intent on them being friends?

Was it because he was the first person she saw after doing the Cupid Stupid Dance?

But that didn't matter.

The man danced like a dream, leaving her shocked. When she thought of him, a redneck always came to mind.

"You still play a mean game of Tomb Raider?"

"Absolutely," she said with confidence. It was still her favorite game, though she had learned others. The memory of how she had beat him at a tournament so long ago returned. Best to keep that to herself, so as not to hurt his fragile ego.

When the song ended, he took her by the hand. "Come on. I owe you a drink to make up for all those years of fighting."

Not to be out done, she smiled. "And I'll buy the second round."

"All right," he said. "What are we drinking?"

"Anything other than champagne. How about if we do tequila shots?"

"What?" he asked, stopping and staring at her.

"Why not? Are you not man enough? I double-dog dare you," she said.

Shaking his head, they continued to the bar. There, he ordered two shots of the potent alcohol.

"On the count of three," he said, holding up his liquor-filled shot glass.

Why had she dared him?

Yes, she liked the taste of tequila, but she knew the alcohol could hit you hard.

They slammed their glasses down on the table, both emptied at the same time. She giggled as the liquor began working through her bloodstream.

"Let's do that again," she said, pulling out some dollar bills. "Bartender! Two more."

They tossed back another shot, and once again, she laughed.

"Come on," he said, grabbing her by the arm and dragging her towards the floor.

This time the music was a slow romantic love song, and he hauled her in close. He melded her body to his, and she wondered what was she doing dancing with the enemy. The warmth of the liquor relaxed her, and she enjoyed every inch of his hard body.

This needed to end.

When the song ended, he led her back to the bar where they stood gazing at one another. The wedding, the laughter, the fun atmosphere, the alcohol all combined to lower her resistance.

Time to go to her room, but she felt reckless tonight. Everything was changing, and she didn't want the party to stop.

"People are looking at us as if they can't believe they're seeing us together," she said, grinning at him.

"Let's give them something to talk about," he said.

Suddenly, he reached out and pulled her in his arms. His lips came towards hers, and she braced herself. At their touch, she was stunned at the warmth they generated as they moved over her mouth. Shock radiated through her, but then heat like a racing train, scorched her body.

She was kissing her arch enemy. She was kissing the man she had hated since junior high. And she didn't want tonight to end.

The touch of his mouth was warm, and she liked the way he tasted of alcohol and cake and forbidden dreams.

"Get a room," someone said, as they walked by.

They came apart, and she gazed at him in awe.

That was some kiss! An unforgettable kiss.

Now what were they supposed to do?

They were making up, but that didn't include making out like a couple of teenagers.

Yet, tonight was a celebration of her sister's wedding.

He ordered more tequila shots, and though she knew she shouldn't, she went ahead and downed the liquor.

"I bet I can still beat you at Tomb Raider," she taunted.

"No doubt," he said. "I haven't played the game in years."

A song from their childhood boomed over the loudspeakers, and he pulled her out onto the dance floor again. Everything about tonight seemed to be pushing them together. They were giggling like two kids when they made their way back to the bar.

People stared at them in disbelief, their feud widely known.

"Remember our favorite television show *Friends*?" he asked. "Remember when Rachel and Ross got married in Vegas? I dare you to shock them all and do a fake wedding with me."

A phony ceremony would be fun. Something to remember their night of forgiving one another. There it was; a dare. A taunt. Oh, how she wanted to tell him no, but something compelled her not to.

"I'm marrying a millionaire Prince Charming, so no, we can't have a real marriage." She glanced around the room, her head spinning, and noticed people whispering and pointing at them.

They couldn't believe their eyes the two of them were drinking and dancing together.

The urge to stun them even more overcame her. "Why not. Let's do this."

"Maybe Elvis would marry us."

"Let's go find him," she said, glancing around at the party which was rapidly winding down. The bride and groom had left hours ago. Her sister, Heather, had disappeared, and was probably up in the room, no doubt studying.

"We've got to hurry," he said. "It's eleven-thirty."

"One more tequila shot of courage," she said, with a laugh.

They downed the last bit of liquor, and suddenly, the alcohol slammed into her. Maybe drinking this much hadn't been her wisest decision.

"Let's go," she said, and the floor seemed to come up to meet her.

Nathan's arm reached out and grabbed her.

Why did she like his touch so much?

She turned and faced him and leaned into him, kissing her arch enemy and wondering why his kiss felt so good.

He broke the kiss, his voice tense. "Let's go get fake married."

"Yes, by Elvis," she said.

CHAPTER SIX

*N*athan awoke to the sound of shrieking. He sat straight up in bed and immediately regretted the quick motion. His head pounded, and his stomach was riding a roller coaster, and any second now, he would go rushing into the bathroom.

The shrill screaming didn't stop, and he turned to see a very naked Caitlyn standing and staring down at the marriage license.

"No, no, no," she kept repeating. "This can't be real."

Well, damn, he'd meant to hide that from her before they went to bed. When they'd reached his hotel room, the clothes had quickly been shed, and they'd tumbled into bed with one another.

No, he hadn't planned on a wedding night, but his new wife had insisted they consummate their union, and who was he to argue.

"Caitlyn," he groaned. "Please stop."

"You son of a bitch," she screamed wheeling around to face him. "You tricked me. This was supposed to be a fake wedding. This paper shows we're married. You hate me. You did this to humiliate me, didn't you?"

Oh, grimany, the woman was turning this all against him.

"No, I didn't. But I need a wife."

"And you think I would marry you for real? Are you crazy?"

At that moment his logical brain screamed he needed to be committed for marrying her and drinking too much.

"Well, I'm not going to be your wife, do you understand me," she yelled. "A fake wedding, and now this legal paper, which appears real to me! Last night was supposed to be fun, nothing permanent."

Tears streamed down her face, making his stomach cringe with remorse.

What had they done?

"No, I don't want to be married to you. No! Just *no*! I want a millionaire, or a billionaire, for a husband. Someone I meet in St. Tropez, not a loser gamer like yourself."

Now that angered him.

What she didn't know was she had just helped him become wealthy, if he could convince her to stay with him for ninety-one days. But he wasn't going to give her the satisfaction of knowing he would be a rich man. Especially after she called him a loser gamer.

"That's not what you said when we reached the courthouse."

"Last night was a joke. A fake marriage."

"Until you decided to make it real," he said.

At the time, the amount of alcohol she'd consumed was way over the legal limit. Even though that had helped him in the long run, guilt ate at him at how he'd used her to obtain what he needed. Somehow, he would make this up to her.

"I did not," she exclaimed. "Never, would I do this. *Never.*"

"Excuse me, but *you* said let's make it real, so we can have sex. You said you did not believe in having sex unless you were married."

That was not a lie. She *had* said those words, which shocked him.

"Yes, but I was saving myself for my Prince Charming."

Too late.

What he remembered of their joining had been spontaneous and combustible. Something he'd never experienced before. If he were lucky, he hoped they would do it again soon.

"This can't be real," she said, starting to sob. "How could I have screwed up my life so badly?"

"Tequila?" he admitted, his head pounding.

Suddenly, she threw the empty bottle of champagne at him, but he ducked, and the bottle bounced against the headboard, before rolling to the floor.

"Last night, you were thrilled we said I do. Last night, you were happy."

"Last night, I was *drunk*! From the time we left the hotel, my memory is nothing. Yes, I knew we were looking for a wedding chapel, but that's all I remember."

And they'd found one. Married by an Elvis impersonator, they ran out of the building, amid wedding bells and flower petals, laughing and barely able to keep their hands off each other.

They rushed back to his hotel room, where they spent the night consummating their union, taking advantage of one another, and making the marriage real.

Only this morning, she remembered nothing of what happened.

"Listen to me. Last night was one of the best nights of my life," he said softly.

She began to sob. Grabbing her clothes, she ran into the bath-room and slammed the door shut. Feeling like a fool, he hurried to the door and tried to talk to her calmly.

"Caitlyn, it's not as bad as you think," he said. "We're going to have fun together."

Loud gut-wrenching sobs filled the air, and a long and drawn out, "*No!*" could be heard a few times.

"Let's give our marriage a chance," he said, talking through the door.

"*No*! You'll never be my Prince Charming," she cried.

With a yank, she opened the bathroom door, and he almost fell in on her. "Stop! Listen to me."

"Get out of my way," she ordered, pushing him to the side in order to walk out the door. "This marriage will be annulled. I'm going to talk to Heather and see what I can do to end this farce of a union. We will never be married for real."

"We already are."

Great sobs escaped her, and she grabbed her purse. Just as she reached for the license, he took the document.

"Oh no, this stays with me."

That piece of paper would prove he was married. Somehow, he needed to convince her to keep this wedding intact for at least ninety-one days. Right now was not the time. Clearly, she refused to listen to him.

"Keep the damn thing. That means nothing to me. You'll be hearing from my attorney."

Standing there in the nude in front of her, she realized for the first time he had no clothes on, no sheet, *nothing*.

Groaning, she turned away from him and headed towards the door, dressed in her bridesmaid dress, and her wedding finery.

It was then he remembered the DVD they purchased.

"Hey, if you don't believe we're married, the ceremony is on the DVD we bought."

"Screw you, Nathan! Why you did this to me, I don't know, but I'm going to make your life a living hell. Do you understand me?"

After last night, he had no doubts she could torment him. Last night, she'd driven him to ecstasy and beyond, and today, the thought of their wedding night left him eager to try again. Not to mention, the torture she was capable of inflicting upon him.

"I'm certain you'll do your best," he replied, as she walked out and slammed the door behind her.

Well, that certainly had not gone like he'd hoped. Maybe she would feel differently later.

CHAPTER SEVEN

*C*aitlyn burst through the door to the hotel room she shared with her sister.

"Where have you been? I've been worried sick," Heather said. "Five minutes more, and I was going to call Mom and Dad and tell them you were missing."

She burst into tears. "I got married last night!"

"*What?* To whom?"

"Nathan Greene. He tricked me. Please help me, Heather. This marriage must be annulled as soon as possible."

Heather stood there staring at her, her mouth open. "Dear God. The Cupid Superstition really is true, for you to have married *him*."

"*No!* It can't be."

Walking to Caitlyn, her sister wrapped her arms around her. "Calm down. Deep breaths. Our car leaves for the airport in an hour. Once we return to Texas, I'll do some research and see how we go about annulling this, if that's really what you want."

With a sigh, Caitlyn stepped back. "*Of course* it's what I want. You *know* my five-year plan. You *know* I'm trying to save enough money for my St Tropez vacation."

The urge to shed the bridesmaid dress overwhelmed her as she started to tug at the zipper.

How could she ever look at this dress again, without thinking she wore this lovely gown the night she lost her mind.

"Tell me what happened. How did you and Nathan end up married?"

For the next five minutes she tried to remember everything about last night to tell her sister. In the retelling, more of the night came to her, and she gasped as she remembered the two of them laughing as they created their fake marriage. Only the wedding wasn't a fake. It was real.

"Instead of tequila making me take my clothes off, it made me into a married woman. How could I be so stupid?"

Shaking her head, Heather stared at in wonder. "Of all the lame-brained things you've done in your life, this one tops the cake. How are you going to keep this a secret?"

Oh, my God, if her family found out, her father would go ballistic, and her mother would be so disappointed.

"I don't know, but please help me! Mother and Daddy can't find out I married the man I hate. No one can learn we're wed."

"And you think he's going to keep this quiet?"

"Aargh, I hope so!" Tears rolled down her cheeks. "My life is ruined. How can I marry a rich man if I'm already married?"

What was she thinking and how had this gone from a fake marriage to a real one?

The vague memory of them reaching the courthouse just before midnight sifted into her brain like mud going through a sifter. They were told that, unless they signed the documents and the minister filed the certificate, the wedding wouldn't be legitimate.

How had Nathan persuaded her into signing the form making this real?

How?

"Go take a shower while I pack your bags."

"My head is pounding from all the tequila I drank. And now I wrecked my life. All my dreams, my plans, *squashed* by one night of recklessness."

No wonder she and Nathan were enemies.

How could she be so stupid as to marry the one man who disliked her so much? They were adversaries, and she'd believed him when he said he wanted to bury the hatchet.

No, he wanted to take the hatchet out and chop her head off with the weapon.

Heather pushed her towards the bathroom. "Oh no, you smell of tequila and..." Her sister's face went white. "Dear God! You slept with him, didn't you?"

The memory of the two of them in bed wrenched sobs from her. Great gulping bouts of ugly crying. *"Yes!* Last night with Nathan was the best sex I have ever experienced. The absolute most wonderful night. *Why Nathan?"*

Stunned, her sister took her by the arm. "Please tell me you used protection. Please."

"Yes, we did. But Heather he's not what I want in life. Yet I'm married to him."

"You should have thought of that sooner."

"It was supposed to be a fake marriage. Somehow, it became real."

"Do you remember if the officiant filed a wedding certificate or the license?"

"No... My memory is so foggy and unclear. Why did I drink so much alcohol?"

As Heather tried to move her towards the bathroom and the shower, she turned and grabbed her arm. "Promise me you'll help me. Promise me."

"Of course I will." With a groan, she said, "Two of my sisters, married on the same day. Dear God, what is this world coming to?"

"Oh Whitney is going to be so mad. Believe me, I didn't plan on stealing her big day, honestly."

With an ache gripping her chest, unlike anything she had ever experienced before, tears welled up in her eyes. Once she got beneath the water's spray, she promised herself a good cry.

"She's on her honeymoon. Whitney never has to learn about this," Heather said. "Let's just keep this secret between us. Once we're home, I'll do the research and start the annulment proceedings."

The tears refused to wait, and Caitlyn began to cry again. "Oh, Heather, what would I do without you? You're my lifesaver."

"Get in the shower; you'll feel better. You're going to need to act normal in front of Mom and Dad. Mother can be very suspicious. So go put on your happy face."

That would be damn near impossible. The plane would be filled with members from the wedding party, and friends and family, and–

Oh dear God!

What was she going to do?

"I'm not feeling very happy. In fact, I think I'm going to be sick."

Nausea roiled through her stomach, her head pounded, and she wanted to die.

"Caitlyn, you need a keeper."

A sob escaped as tears flowed from her eyes. "Yes, all my dreams of marrying a rich husband have been ruined by one night in Vegas."

CHAPTER EIGHT

*C*aitlyn sat in her airplane seat, praying for takeoff, the pounding in her head doing the tango. At the airport, she avoided speaking to Nathan, though he repeatedly tried to gain her attention. But Heather hovered over her like a protective hen and kept them separated. While her mother stared at her as if she knew something was wrong.

When they boarded the plane, she noticed Nathan was sitting in first class and groaned. The same area as her parents. As she walked down the aisle, she averted her gaze.

Three hours.

Once they landed, she would do everything to keep him from interfering in her life.

"Did you see that?" she asked Heather. "He's in first class with Mother and Daddy."

"Yes," Heather said. "Not good."

"You don't think he'll tell them, do you?"

"No," her sister said, as they reached their seats. "Not unless he wants our father to go off on him right here."

Their father was not known for his diplomacy, but rather, his frank protective nature regarding his daughters. Especially Caitlyn, who he deemed a lost soul in need of rescuing. Heather was the smart one, as far as he was concerned, and Whitney and he clashed on everything.

The passengers all boarded and placed their luggage in the overhead bins, then located their seats. Caitlyn sat thinking she would never drink tequila again.

"I'm dying," Caitlyn said. "Maybe my death would be for the best."

"No, I thought we'd do tequila shots all the way back to Dallas," Heather responded.

The idea made nausea rise in her already battered stomach.

"Really? I'm at death's door, and you're making jokes?"

Her sister grinned. "Just trying to remind you how you screwed up, so you don't drink like that again."

The two of them gazed out the window while the stewardess went through her departure routine. Soon, the airplane backed out of the gate, and they taxied down the runway, heading back to Texas.

Whitney and Aaron had left early this morning to fly to Los Angeles, where they were catching a cruise to Hawaii for their honeymoon.

The wedding party had flown out together, but several members stayed behind to enjoy the sights of Vegas. Owning her own beauty shop, Caitlyn needed to return home and get back to work. Heather needed to return to continue studying for the bar exam, and their parents were not fans of the Vegas scene, so they headed back as well.

As soon as the plane reached cruising altitude, Caitlyn leaned her chair back, determined to rest and ease her pounding head. If she pretended to sleep all the way to Dallas, maybe they would all leave her alone to think about how she could untangle the mess she'd created.

Suddenly, she heard her father's voice clearly from where he sat in First Class. "She did *what!*"

Oh no!

Caitlyn's eyes flew open.

"Did you hear that?" she asked her sister.

"Yes," Heather replied, as they both peered down the aisle towards the commotion.

The seat belt sign went off, and she could see her father rising from his seat.

"Oh shit!" she said. "Here he comes. The rat bastard told him."

Like a man on a mission, her father marched down the aisle towards where they sat, his face red, his eyes flashing with anger. Coming to a halt at their seats, he glared at Caitlyn.

"Did you marry Nathan Greene last night?

With her head pounding, and her heart thumping in her chest with a Congo beat, she swallowed her fear. "It was supposed to be a fake marriage. For fun."

"It's not fake!" he yelled. "He showed me the marriage license. Of all the stupid stunts you've ever pulled, this one is the worst!"

"Sir, you need to take your seat," the stewardess said from behind the furious man.

Could her embarrassment get any worse?

The whole plane was now staring at them, and her father only raised his voice louder.

"Can't you see I'm busy telling my daughter she's a fool!"

The flight attendant gave him her meanest look, but Caitlyn's father ignored her, turned back to his daughter, and continued his rant.

"You have hated this man all your life, yet you *married* him? Were you drunk!"

What was she supposed to say?

"I'm going to talk to my law professor about how to annul the marriage," Heather cut in, trying to calm their father.

"Were you drunk?" their father asked again, ignoring Heather.

"Yes, daddy," Caitlyn said meekly, knowing she'd truly made a real mess of things. "We were drinking tequila."

"Dear God!" he shouted in disbelief. "And you thought marrying your enemy would be funny?"

"Sir, you're going to need to take your seat so we can serve refreshments."

"I don't give a damn about refreshments; let me speak to my idiot daughter!"

The only thing worse thing that could happen, was if she began to throw up...something which was very much imminent. One good bounce, and she would be using the vomit bag.

"We'll speak about this when we arrive in Dallas," she said wondering if she could get away with murder. What would her life be like to live as a widow? In prison?

Just then, a man from the back approached. "Sit down, sir, or I'll tell the pilot to turn this plane around and have you removed."

"Go sit down, daddy," she pleaded, knowing things had the potential to get a lot worse.

In fear, she watched her father glare at the man, who she assumed must be the air marshal. Her father gave her one last searing look, one which should have lit her hair on fire. "I hope you're happy; your mother is sitting up front, crying. We're not through discussing this, young lady."

She mentally groaned with the realization they had an upcoming, two-hour drive from Dallas once they landed. They would all be in the car, packed together, and she would be forced to listen to him tell her how she'd completely wrecked her life.

And unless she got this sham of a marriage annulled, she would have destroyed all her dreams. She didn't need anyone telling her this.

With a whirl, her father turned around and walked back up the aisle, the passengers all staring at them, and the dysfunctional family spectacle they'd just witnessed.

Why did Nathan tell her father?

What was the purpose behind him causing all this unnecessary drama, when she told him she was going to have the marriage annulled?

"Well, I guess we know he's not going to keep your marriage a secret," Heather said.

Her sister's words pushed her over the edge, and Caitlyn grabbed the barf bag and threw up.

Was there any way off this plane?

Any way at all?

Jump out a window?

Get sucked out through the toilet?

In this moment, she would even welcome death.

In two hours, when they landed, she would let Nathan know her thoughts and feelings in a very loud, and very unmistakable way.

But when she walked off the plane, Nathan was nowhere to be found.

The chicken walked down the ramp and left her to deal with her father…alone.

CHAPTER NINE

*T*he ride home could best be described as sailing on the Titanic with the iceberg in view. Very few words were said as her father drove them home. In the front seat, her mother softly wept for the entire ride home.

When they finally reached Caitlyn's apartment in Cupid, her father pulled up to the curb and got out of the car.

"Bye, Mom," she told her softly, before climbing out.

The only response she received were even more sobs.

Heather squeezed her hand. "I'll call you as soon as I speak to my professor."

Dread made moving her feet toward the trunk where her father was waiting, after having removed her suitcase, difficult. It was odd he hadn't said much the entire way home. As a matter of fact, the car had been eerily silent.

"You and Nathan are to be at the house tomorrow night for dinner. We will decide how to handle this disaster you've created."

His voice was stern, and she knew better than to argue. This was a demand, not a request.

"Yes, sir."

Rolling her luggage, she walked towards the apartment, her heart heavy, her chest aching with pain over, what had started as a beautiful weekend, having gone horribly wrong. Whitney's wedding would always be remembered as the event where she'd made the biggest mistake of her life.

Her father got back in the vehicle and took off, not even making certain she got into her unit. Walking through the complex, she rounded the corner and saw Nathan standing near her door, obviously waiting for her.

Shaking her head, she stopped and stared at him, swearing beneath her breath.

Could she avoid talking to him?

Probably not. Besides, she wanted to hear his pathetic excuse for tattling to her father.

She strolled up to her apartment, her body rigid, and didn't say a word to him as she inserted her key in the lock and swung open the door. He stood watching her, his arms folded across his chest.

"Come in," she said, and this time, it was she who wasn't asking, but demanding.

He followed her into the apartment, where she turned on him and unleashed her fury.

"Why the hell did you tell my father! Do you know how badly you've ruined my life?"

Yes, her words sounded overly-dramatic, but at the moment, she felt as if everything was coming to an end.

" I didn't want him to learn about our wedding from someone else," he said. "Imagine how angry your father would have been if he learned about our marriage from someone other than us. So I told him. After all, you plan to have the union annulled anyway."

That just showed her how much he didn't understand her father's way of thinking. That man believed marriage was forever, and he would want them to remain together.

"You almost got us kicked off the plane," she said. "The air marshal even threatened to turn the jet back. *The air marshal!*"

"Your father didn't take the news too well," he said. "I'm guessing he's not going to consider me the son-he's-never-had."

His flippant comment enraged her, and the urge to pound him left her body trembling. How could he make light of this situation when everything she ever wanted was at stake?

"Hardly," she said. "So how do we annul this? We're not staying married."

Nathan was quiet for several minutes. "Would you consider waiting ninety-one days?"

Stunned he would even suggest such a thing, she glared at him. "What are you saying? Of course not. This marriage is being annulled right away."

Now was not the time for him to be asking any favors from her. Nope, nada, ain't happening!

"Since we slept together, it will be hard to get an annulment. Which was totally your idea and the reason we're married."

A blush spread across her face, and she gripped her fists, trying to control the outrage. The sex *had* been outstanding though.

Please, she didn't say that aloud, did she?

"You're lying, I would never suggest we make it a real marriage. Never."

"You did."

No, she refused to believe him, because she understood what she wanted. A billionaire she met on the island of St. Tropez.

"I'm not going to do this, but I do want to know why you want me to wait for ninety-one days?"

"For a couple of reasons: We can make certain there are no repercussions from our sleeping together, and I need a wife."

Repercussions?

There better *not* be any repercussions!

Last night, she was sure she remembered them using condoms.

"What?"

"I need someone to play my wife for that long," he said.

"Why?"

"I'm working on a business deal, and I have a good chance of winning, but only if I'm married."

Was this true, or once again, was he lying to her?

"Why should I care whether you receive this contract?"

"I'm willing to pay you to remain married to me for three months."

This must be especially important for him to offer cash for her to stay in the union.

"Please tell me you're not talking forever?"

"No, just until I am awarded the deal, which I should know in ninety days."

This was a strange coincidence.

Would he have deliberately married her just to score this business deal?

How much was he willing give her?

Enough for her to take her dream vacation, where she would meet her real husband?

"Did you do this on purpose so I would marry you?"

A frown spread across his face. "Yes and no," he said. "Yes, I needed a wife. Of all the women at the wedding, you're the only one who interested me. But I didn't know if you would agree. You can lead a horse to water, but you can't make them drink, and all that."

Oh, nice. Not only had he tricked her into marrying him, but he'd planned to try to convince her to wed him. And now, he had the audacity to ask her to *remain* married to him.

Anger sparked like a raging inferno inside her as she walked away to the kitchen, needing some space. She very much wanted to get even with him somehow.

"So you're comparing me to a horse?"

"No, I'm not. You're beautiful and sexy, and when you suggested we make the wedding real, I agreed, knowing it would benefit me."

What a lie! She would never agree to marry him for real.

"Well, how great for you. It kind of screws me though."

She would never want a marriage with this man. *Never*.

Then again, she'd been filled with tequila and only remembered flashes of really hot sex, and laughing and giggling and–

Oh crap, her asking Nathan to marry her!

Why the hell had she done that?

Had it been a joke, or just the alcohol speaking?

Well, it would never last. A handsome, wealthy man waited for her in St. Tropez, but so far, she hadn't been able to afford the vacation.

Could this be her golden ticket?

"Like I said, I'm willing to pay you if you will stay with me for ninety-one days."

" I don't think you can afford me, but if so, fine. Let's do it," she said the words aloud and was surprised her thoughts had so easily slipped out of her mouth.

Stunned, he stared at her. "Really? You'll stay?"

"Why not? The cash I could use to do what I want," she said, wincing inside.

Was she selling herself off to this man to obtain what she wanted?

No, there would be no further hanky-panky. Even though, from the little she remembered, the sex had been outstanding, and well, she'd always had a small crush on Nathan. One she didn't want to recognize.

"Forty thousand dollars," she said thinking that would give her some extra to buy a new wardrobe, and even do some things in the spa. New sinks would be wonderful.

"Agreed," he said immediately.

Startled, she suddenly realized he would have paid more.

"After we've been married ninety-one days, I will pay you forty thousand dollars, and then we can proceed with the divorce proceedings. Is it a deal?"

Nerves gripped Caitlyn's stomach as she gazed at the man.

What in the hell was she doing?

The end result would get her to St. Tropez to meet Mr. Perfect.

Why was she hesitating?

Because she feared her emotions becoming involved with Mr. Wrong.

Still, if she didn't agree, when would she make it to St. Tropez?

"Deal," she said. "We're expected at my parent's house tomorrow night for dinner."

"Oh no. I didn't think about the family."

"How do we handle them? My father will never accept we're going to pretend to be married for only a certain amount of time."

A mischievous smile spread across his face. "We play the loving couple. Move into my place, and we're the lovebirds people expect of newlyweds. That way, everyone believes the marriage is real. Right up until D-Day."

Was she crazy?

The sane, rational part of her said run.

Could she pretend they were madly in love?

"How do I know you can compensate me the money? If you double-cross me, I will make your life a living hell."

"My lawyer will draw up an agreement. The only requirement is that you must stay until day ninety-one, and then I'll pay you."

It would be enough cash to get her to St. Tropez for her luxury dream vacation and then some. Still, there were so many loose ends.

"How do we explain today?"

"When we sat down, we realized how much we cared about each other and decided to give the marriage a chance."

"That's not the truth."

"No, but it's as close as we can came to the actual truth."

Caitlyn shook her head.

Why did this feel like she were digging an even deeper hole for herself?

CHAPTER TEN

*N*athan's insides were quaking like a seven point earthquake as they stood outside the door to her parent's house. Mr. Beckett was not someone who played nice especially when it came to his daughters.

On the airplane, Nathan feared the man was going to punch him. At the time, it seemed like a good idea to tell her parents, but their reactions stunned him. Especially, when Mr. Beckett screamed at him, sending the stewardesses rushing into first class.

As soon as that plane landed he had taken off, leaving Caitlyn to deal with her family. Until the man calmed down, he didn't want to be near him.

Now they were here to face them together. He turned and gazed at her, she appeared so nervous. "Are you ready?"

"No," she said. "Let's just go home. We can tell them later."

They had spent the better part of the day moving her into a room in his home It made him feel good that she called it home, but somehow he didn't think she thought of his place as her home, yet.

SYLVIA MCDANIEL

"That would be disrespectful. We need to do things right," he said.

"Like getting drunk and getting married in Vegas was doing things right?"

A smile spread across his face. What could he say, she was right. They had acted out and ended up married.

"No, but we're doing better now."

In his hands he had flowers for her mother and a bottle of wine for her father. What kind of gifts did you take to your mother and father-in-law.

Leaning down he kissed her on the mouth and she pulled back frowning. "What was that for?"

"Good luck. Now remember we are so happy. We've kissed and made up and we're going to live our life together. We're on our honeymoon."

She rolled her eyes at him. "I've never been a good actress."

"Well tonight, you're going to put on the best performance of your life."

She rang the door bell and within seconds her family stood there gazing at the two of them, with daggers in their eyes.

"Mom," she said giving her a hug.

Heather's brows raised at the sight of the flowers and the bottle of wine.

"Mrs. Beckett, these are for you," Nathan said handing her the flowers.

Her mother took them politely, but she was cold. "Flowers won't make up for marrying my daughter."

"No, they don't, but I'm hoping they will at least make you think better of me."

"That's going to take some work," her mother said taking the flowers from his hand and heading towards the kitchen.

Nathan wasn't doing very well. Maybe he would fare better with the father.

"Mr. Beckett, Caitlyn told me this was your favorite wine," he said handing him the bottle.

"Thank you. Come in young man. Mother will join us in the study shortly. You two have some things to answer for. Caitlyn, I've already contacted an attorney to clean up this mess."

She whirled around and stared at Nathan in fear.

"Daddy, we don't want to annul the marriage."

The sound of glass breaking in the kitchen, had Heather dashing off to check on their mother.

"Both of you into the study, now," her father said.

This was not going to be easy. Her father was still a man with a chip on his shoulder the size of Gibraltar. But then again, he had married his daughter without his permission, while she was drunk on tequila.

Her father walked around behind his large oak desk and sat in an overstuffed chair. A wall behind him was covered in his degrees, his certificates showing how long he served on the city council and as the Mayor of Cupid.

Her mother slipped in through the door and closed it behind her quietly.

"Heather is going to finish dinner while we talk," she said staring at him. "Tell me young man, you hate my daughter, so why did you marry her?"

The lady didn't hold anything back, going straight for his jugular.

"Sometimes hate is hiding the emotions you're really feeling. While we have had our differences, I've always had a crush on her. Was I ready to say I do? No, but fate seemed to think we were ready."

Part of what he said was true. In fact, really all of it seemed appropriate. While he had hoped to marry Caitlyn in Vegas, it had come together almost like the Cupid statue was directing how things would happen.

"Do you love her," Mrs. Beckett asked and he could see that she was a strong protector of her daughters.

He glanced at Caitlyn and she sent him a secret smile. "I'd say I'm falling in love with her. We had no intention on getting married that night, but what was supposed to be a fake wedding, quickly turned real."

Her father frowned. "I don't know why anyone would want to do a fake wedding. That makes no sense."

"We were pretending, Daddy. Just like you use to pretend with me sometimes when we played dolls."

The man was not buying her explanation as he shook his head. "You're a little old for make believe. Especially, when it comes to such a serious subject. And I am so disappointed in how much you drank at your sister's wedding. Tequila shots?"

They were both quiet as he reprimanded them on the dangers of drinking. "You're too old to be acting this way, Caitlyn. So how are you two going to get out of this mess?"

For the first time, Nathan felt like they might weather the storm. He glanced over at Caitlyn smiled and took her trembling hand. "We're not."

Mrs. Beckett gasped and even Mr. Beckett leaned forward. "What did you just say young man?"

"Last night we talked, after we both calmed down, and well, we've decided we're going to give this marriage a try."

"Oh, no,"' Mrs. Beckett said. "This will never work. Do you know her dreams?"

Stunned she would be so against him, Nathan gazed at the woman. "Whose dreams?"

"My daughter's, of course. Her plans since she graduated from college have been to marry a rich man. That's all we've heard about is her five year plan to marry a wealthy man."

Fear spiraled through Nathan and gripped his stomach. If she knew the real reason he married her daughter, she would understand they were both searching to make their first millions. If they could keep things together for just eighty-nine days, he would be a wealthy man.

But he didn't want a wife who remained married to him because of his wealth.

"What is your financial situation young man?"

"I work for Aaron for his foundation and I also have an app that is making me a nice amount of money each month."

"An App?" Her father asked.

"Yes, a computer app that gamers use to get to the next level in games."

Mr. Beckett frowned and he knew he didn't approve of gamers.

"Can you support my daughter?"

"Yes, I can," he said thinking if his daughter remained married to him, they would have an easy life. But he didn't want her to know about the money. Especially, after learning about her dream.

"It's not like I'm going to stop working?" Caitlyn said. "I have my business."

"Your business is never going to earn you a lot of money. And you have expensive tastes," her father reprimanded.

"I'm sorry, my little business is letting me live a good life," she said her voice rising.

Nathan sensed her tense and knew this particular argument had been going on for a while. Somehow he needed to calm the situation. "I have the wedding CD if you'd like to see our ceremony."

Caitlyn jerked towards him and he could tell she would rather he had not mentioned the evidence of their wedding.

She hadn't seen it, yet, but Nathan watched it earlier this afternoon.

Her mother seized on the opportunity to see their wedding. "Put it in the disc player, Milton."

The man frowned at his wife, but got up and took the CD from him. Soon the ceremony was playing on their television.

Nathan glanced at Caitlyn who stared at the screen. Her mother began to cry and her father frowned.

Then she said the words he wanted everyone to hear, but especially Caitlyn.

"Let's make this a real wedding," she giggled and threw her arms around him. "No one will believe we're married."

Her father turned and glared at her and her mother continued to cry.

On the television screen, Nathan nodded and the ceremony began. As they said I do, they laughed through out the ceremony like they were the happiest couple in love with each other.

At the end, the kiss they shared, Nathan would never forget. At that moment, he suddenly had doubts about what they were doing, because he feared that in eighty-nine days, this woman would own his heart.

CHAPTER ELEVEN

Caitlyn hated lying. Yes, they were going to remain married, but only for ninety-one days. Sitting on the couch in his house, she gazed around at the home, surprised at the elegance of his living quarters. The house, an older remodeled Victorian, was quite nice.

"Who did the remodel on your house?"

"Chloe Lawrence," he said. "Not too terribly long after she had her first baby with Drew."

The preacher's daughter was well-known for restoring old houses and also for doing the Cupid Stupid Dance and marrying the bad boy in town.

"She did a great job remodeling," she said, glancing around.

"I thought tonight went well."

Turning, she gave him a look which clearly said she disagreed. "Oh yes, it went so well, tomorrow morning I expect a phone call from Heather, saying meet me for lunch."

Her smart sister would be the hardest person to convince Nathan was what Caitlyn wanted, especially after talking to her about her dreams of marrying a billionaire.

"It will take time for everyone to believe we're together."

Oh, he didn't know her sister. Or her mother, for that matter. Those two women could be as stubborn as they come.

"Heather is studying to be a lawyer, and after we left Vegas, was researching annulments. She's going to ask me why I changed my mind. You can't bullshit her with hearts and flowers. She's too smart to fall for lies."

The man laughed. "Tell her my charming ways made you come over to the dark side."

Charming ways?

How had he convinced her to make this marriage real?

She'd been drunk, had she even realized what she'd been saying?

Sadly, Caitlyn had no recollection of that part of the ceremony.

How could she remain angry at him if *she* had been the one who'd insisted on making their vows permanent?

If she hadn't seen herself say the words on the video, she would never have believed him. Still, how did she find herself in such a mess.

"And do you believe my mother is buying into our marriage? All these years, you were my enemy. Mother knew we hated each other, and she's not going to accept we've suddenly fallen in love." Caitlyn shook her head. "Her first question will be to ask if I'm pregnant!"

Oh, yes, her mother would be hinting, searching, and eventually, would come right out and ask if her first grandbaby was on the way.

Nathan chuckled, though the idea of her expecting seemed to almost frighten him, because his voice sounded quite tense all of a sudden.

"You're not though…right?"

With a glance at him, she said, "From what I remember of our wedding night, we used condoms, so we should be all right."

A sigh escaped from him. "Good."

"We've not discussed the possibility."

"Not going to happen," he said.

"Right," she agreed, thinking that would be the absolute worst thing.

Sitting across the couch from her, he turned and stared. "Is it true you've always wanted to marry a wealthy man?"

"Yes," she said. "If I'd seen Aaron first, he would have been mine. But I didn't, and he's now married to my sister. No one else in Cupid is that rich. So I'm just going to have to look elsewhere for my husband to be."

Shaking his head, he glanced away.

"Do you have a problem with that? Because if so, let me know right now and this deal is off."

The reason she'd decided to remain with him was to earn the money for her trip to St. Tropez. Sun, sex, romance, and a man looking for forever.

With a jerk his head turned back to her. "It seems desperate. What if a man said he would only marry a gorgeous blonde, instead of a redhead? What about guys like me.? Aren't you overlooking us?"

Her brows rose as she tipped her head down and gazed at him. "No, I'm not overlooking men like you. I'm going after what I want. A poor schmuck whose wife must work one or two jobs, while taking care of their babies, is not the kind of life I want."

Why was it wrong to fall in love and marry a man with money, instead of someone like Nathan?

"What if you fall for a poor man?"

"I don't date men who are not wealthy" she said firmly.

"Wow, just…wow," he said. "So an ordinary guy has no chance with you?"

"That's right," she said. "The money I make from pretending to be your wife is just enough to get me to St Tropez, where I will meet and fall for my billionaire bachelor."

He started laughing aloud. "Do you think a rich man is going to say 'I do' with a small-town girl, with no trust fund? Doubtful."

Ouch!

That was her biggest fear. Not that she wasn't pretty enough, but rather because she would bring no money to aid in the building of their empire.

"No, they will fall in love with me because Beauty and Brains will get the job done."

His face fell, as if she'd hurt him, and for some reason, that knowledge left her feeling sad. Bringing up their past like that had just been her attempt to lighten the mood; she hadn't meant for it to ruin their time together, or especially, to hurt him.

"Most of these men have prearranged marriages. The wife comes with just as big a bank account as the man. Their union is more of a merger than an actual marriage," he told her.

Not all wealthy men insisted on a woman with a large bank account. Caitlyn felt confident she would find the right husband for her on the island. All she needed to do was find a way there.

"Tell me about this contract you're trying to obtain and need a wife to reel in the business."

His body jerked, almost as if she'd electrocuted him with her words, but then he quickly recovered, and said, "What? Oh, yeah, the contract. Sorry, but I was mentally back in junior high for a moment, wondering what kind of friends we'd have been if we'd never gotten involved in that damned class president race."

"It probably still wouldn't have happened," she said. "We always seem to clash."

However, now they were no longer were they clashing, but rather, they seemed to work together very well. *Too* well, and that frightened her.

He didn't mention anything about the contract, and she didn't want to press him.

"It's getting late. Time for me to turn in for the night."

"You sure you don't want to sleep with me?"

Fear gripped her chest. The thought of sleeping beside him was tempting. The sex between them had been fantastic, and she was sure sleeping together would only lead to them doing the horizontal mambo once again. If she slept with her husband, the lovemaking would lead to her heart being involved, and that was simply something she had to avoid at all costs.

"We *are* married," he reminded her.

"And the sex was hot. Almost too hot. Why ruin a wonderful memory?"

" I didn't think you remembered any of it."

"Some parts I do," she said, as she got to her feet. "Goodnight, Nathan. Sleep well...*alone*."

CHAPTER TWELVE

*C*aitlyn didn't go into the salon before ten, so they were enjoying breakfast together when her cellphone rang at eight o'clock the next morning. When, he noticed the name on the screen a grin spread across his face.

"You were right," he told her.

As she'd said, her mother was the first to call and check on her.

"Good morning, Mother," she said.

"Are you all right this morning?"

"I'm fine," she said. "I only had to dodge his knife a few times last night."

Silence filled the airways.

"That's not funny, Caitlyn."

"You're right. Does daddy snore? My husband snores."

Again, silence, as her mother tried to process the fact her daughter now slept with a man. "No, your father does not."

"Oh you're so lucky," she said, as Nathan glared at her.

"Dear, I must ask…are you pregnant?"

For a moment, she considered not responding and just leave

her mother to wonder anxiously, but that would be mean, and she didn't need anyone speculating about a possible pregnancy.

"No, Mother. No grandbabies are in your future from me. In fact, they are part of the ten-year plan, not the five-year plan."

"Oh, Caitlyn, you and your plans. Someday you're going to realize how important just living your life can be. And your plans were foiled, so you need to rethink what you're doing."

The words stung, but her mother was right; marrying Nathan had not been in her plans at all. "Have a great day, Mother. Bye."

Hanging up, she sighed.

Why was her mother the one person who could create doubts in Caitlyn's mind about her choices?

In less than five minutes after ending the call with her mother, Caitlyn's sister, Heather, called. Since they lived in the same house, she should have told her to hand the phone over, but she didn't think about it until the second call.

"Can you do lunch today?"

Caitlyn checked her appointment book. "As long as it's a late one."

"All right. I'll meet you at the Cupid restaurant at one o'clock."

Later that day, Caitlyn slowly strolled down the street to the diner, when all she wanted to do was turn around and run back to her shop. At least there she had a sanctuary only customers invaded.

When she walked in the door, the owner, Taylor Jones, glanced at her hand.

Dear God, the news had spread already?

Heather waved from where she was sitting. "There she is."

"Enjoy your lunch," Taylor said, and dashed back into her office at the sound of a baby's cry.

This luncheon was going to be a test, she realized, as she slid into the booth. "Are you recovered from Vegas yet?"

A frown spread across her sister's face. "No, and I'm not going to ask that question of you, because I'm certain you must be reeling from the fact you're married."

It was true. There was no denying her claim.

"Yes," she said.

"Let's be honest with one another. You hate this guy. Please explain to me what you're doing?"

She and Nathan had agreed to keep the details of their situation between themselves, because if the company offering him the contract learned the truth, he would lose the offer, and all of this would be for naught.

"Everything is like what we told Mom and Dad After we talked about the wedding, we kissed and made up, and decided to give marriage a try."

Leaning back in the booth, Heather stared. "You're lying. I know you're lying because you would never marry a man who wasn't worth millions. From what I've seen, I doubt Nathan has enough cash to get through next week."

Now seeing his home, watching him work and overhearing his conversations, Caitlyn was beginning to question her earlier thoughts regarding his wealth. Maybe he wasn't rich enough to marry *her*, but he did indeed have some money. Enough he was able to sign a contract to pay her forty thousand dollars at least.

"You should see where he lives. Actually, you should see where *we* live. Nathan owns a very nice Victorian home, completely updated."

Stunned, Heather glared at her. "Did an alien abduct you? Where is my sister?"

A giggle escaped Caitlyn, and after the tension of the last few days, it felt wonderful to laugh. "I don't think so. No weird lights or intimate probes. Well..."

"That's what I thought."

"Heather, everything is going to be fine. Trust me."

Her sister shook her head as she stared at her. "I'm worried about you. After you arrived back at the hotel room, you were insistent on getting this wedding annulled. When we got home, you changed your mind. It makes no sense. Especially since you always claimed to hate that man."

Her sister didn't know it was only a superficial hatred, and beneath their irreverent banter, she also had a crush on him.

Did that make her crazy?

"Who knows…maybe the Cupid Dance Superstition is true. Maybe it changed my heart and made me look at him in a different light."

With a shake of her head, Heather asked, her eyes wide with disbelief, "What about St. Tropez? A billionaire husband? Does none of that matter anymore?"

How could she respond?

That was the reason she was going along with this fake marriage to the man she once–superficially–hated, even though she was really enjoying herself with him. And they had over eighty-eight days left together. Then she would fly away while he started the annulment proceedings, she would be locating her dream man.

With a sigh, she smiled. "Only if he decides not to take me on a real honeymoon."

"Oh, dear, you have been invaded by a life force I don't recognize."

The waitress arrived at their table. "What can I get for you ladies."

"If you order meatloaf, I'm taking you to a doctor."

Caitlyn burst out laughing. Her most hated dish was one of the specials that day.

"The Cobb salad for me," she said with a smile at Heather.

"Give me the meatloaf," Heather said, "with a side of Scotch. After this weekend, I can't take much more and need some kind of insulation."

"Just don't order tequila."

"Yeah, I know. Look what happened to you! You ended up married."

CHAPTER THIRTEEN

*a*s soon as Caitlyn left, he picked up the phone and called his uncle's lawyer.

"Mr. Shanker please," he said when the receptionist answered.

In a matter of minutes, the man himself was on the line.

"This is Nathan Greene. I wanted to let you know I got married last weekend."

Silence filled the air for at least a full thirty seconds.

"Ahem, well, ah... All right. Send me a copy of the license. Even though you've not been married for long, the clock began ticking the moment your marriage became official. Once you reach the ninety-one days, I'll transfer you the money."

"I wish he hadn't forced me into marriage, but I'm glad I'm doing something he would have liked."

The lawyer laughed. "Your Uncle John was quite the character and wanted you to be happy. Congratulations on your wedding; I hope she's a good woman."

"Thank you," Nathan said, then hung up.

Next, he called his cousin, Jim. "Hey, man, I wanted to tell you I got married this past weekend."

Again, silence filled the line. Obviously, no one had expected him to marry.

"You did this because of the will, didn't you?"

"I've known Caitlyn for many years. We were out in Vegas at her sister's wedding and we snuck off and had a private ceremony of our own."

"Congratulations. This means you receive all the money," he said, but his tone seemed to be a bit off to Nathan.

"This means I'm a happy married man," Nathan answered in return.

Why hadn't his uncle willed any of his money to the rest of the family?

Obviously he had his reasons, but what were they?

"Good luck, man. I hope this is worth it for you."

"Thanks, Jim," he said, before hanging up. The word of his marriage would soon spread through the family, and he could probably expect the same—or worse—reactions from other members.

Something about money always seemed to bring out the worst in people.

Had it brought out the worst in him?

After all, he had tricked his enemy into marrying him.

CHAPTER FOURTEEN

*T*wo weeks later, as the sun was beginning to sink in the sky, Nathan sat working on information Aaron needed. Soon, his wife would be home.

They had fallen into a routine he actually enjoyed, and he was learning his wife was an excellent cook.

The doorbell rang, and he rose from the computer slowly and crossed the room to answer the door.

There stood Amanda, and suddenly, he realized he'd forgotten all about their bi-weekly dinner date.

"When you didn't show up, I started to get worried," she said.

"Come in," he said, "we need to talk."

Shutting the door behind her, he led her into the family room.

"Something's happened I didn't plan on."

While they weren't technically *dating*, per say, they had been seeing each other once a week for quite a while now and occasionally had sex. No grand passion existed between them, and he always felt as if she were just using him, as he used her.

More than anything though, they were friends.

When she sat down on the coach, he joined her and took her

hand. "Our friendship has meant a lot to me over the years, and I hope you know that. However, things have changed in my life significantly, and, well...this past weekend, I got married."

"You did what! To who?"

He took a deep breath and smiled. "Caitlyn Beckett and I tied the knot late Saturday night after her sister's wedding."

Stunned, she stared at him. "But you hated her just last week!"

"Yeah, well, not anymore," he said.

In fact, he quite enjoyed her company. And if he were honest, he never really hated her. He just felt the need to reciprocate her feelings towards him. Maybe it was his way of protecting himself...and his heart.

"Wow, I don't know what to say," she said. "This was not what I expected to learn tonight."

"I'm sorry for not calling you. But maybe it's better this way that you learned about my marriage directly from me."

After learning about his uncle's money and deciding to pursue Caitlyn, he had forgotten all about his friend Amanda.

Shaking her head, she rose from the couch. "I'm crushed. I'm also happy for you, though she's never who I would have pictured you with."

A grin spread across his face. "Me neither."

Wrapping his arms around her, he pulled her in for a hug and kissed her just as the door opened and Caitlyn walked in.

"What the hell?"

They instantly sprang apart.

CHAPTER FIFTEEN

*H*er arch enemy was kissing her husband, her second arch enemy. How did she handle this? Sure, she could make a scene, but why? She and Nathan were married, but not wed in the sense of they loved each other until death do they part. Their marriage was more of a business arrangement.

Only he was violating his oath of office.

"Amanda, how are you?" she asked trying to be nice, while inside she wanted to pull the young woman's hair out of her head, strand by strand. But why should she care? Why?

"You stole my man," she accused.

"Oh, I didn't know about the two of you," she replied sitting the sacks of groceries down on the counter.

Amanda's eyes glinted like daggers and Caitlyn realized she was upset. It was true, Nathan never said anything about dating anyone.

"Honey, you didn't tell me about Amanda. You told me about your other girlfriends, but if I had known about Amanda..."

The woman turned and glared at him. "Other girlfriends?"

"There was no one else and I apologize for not telling you

about our marriage. It happened so quickly," Nathan said suddenly trying to defend himself.

Amanda grabbed her purse off the couch. "It's best I get going. The only reason I'm here is because Nathan missed our dinner date."

"I'm so sorry, Amanda," Caitlyn said, thinking her husband really did screw up. Leaving a woman sitting at a restaurant alone was an insult. "Men can be so trying."

"Ain't that the truth," Amanda said, as she strode towards the door, where she then turned and gazed at the two of them. "Didn't see this one coming at all. Best of luck to the both of you."

With that, she walked out the door.

Caitlyn begin to hum as she put the groceries she'd purchased away. Why did she experience a little joy in the way her husband squirmed when she mentioned other women? That's what he gets for having a woman over and for her walking in on them kissing.

"I think you enjoyed that little scene."

A quick glance over at him, confirmed his smirky smile. "Who me?"

"Yes, you. You've never gotten along with Amanda."

That was true.

"So you think it's all right for a wife to walk in and see her husband's lips on another woman?"

"No, I didn't say that?"

"How would you like it if you came in and found me making out on the couch with another man?"

"Well, I don't have to worry since you don't date poor men."

That burned. Caitlyn stopped and stared at him Did he want to make this a challenge, because if so, she would and could find someone to make out with her.

"Are you issuing me a challenge? Ask my sister how I react to challenges," she replied squeezing the lettuce a little harder than she intended.

"No," he said. "When my wife walked in the door, I was hugging and giving her a kiss goodbye."

She shoved the bread into the bread box.

"Why didn't you tell me you were dating," she responded trying to keep her growing frustration with him under wraps, but fearing she was doing a lousy job. Why did she care? "Well if I had known we could continue seeing other people while married I would have fired up my online account."

Carefully, she removed the wrapper from the Coconut Cream pie she purchased for tonight's meal. Her intentions had been to come home and fix him a decent meal. But right now, he would be lucky to eat SOS for dinner.

"I'm not sure you would call it a date."

"What? Did you not hear the woman? You stood her up," she said her voice rising. Was the man blind? The woman thought they were dating. Now she probably believed Caitlyn had moved in on her man.

"Now Amanda thinks I broke you guys up by marrying you," she said. "Why didn't you tell me or her?"

"Because frankly, I didn't think we were serious. We've been seeing each other about every other week for the last year, but it would never last."

"Then why didn't you end it with her?"

Why did men like to drag something out when the relationship had no future? Just to continue sleeping with her?

Standing less than a foot from her, he shrugged. "It was convenient"

Wrong thing to say.

With a yank, she grabbed the pie and threw the creamy concoction at his face. "Convenient? No woman wants to be thought of as convenient. Come on, I don't even like Amanda, but I felt bad for her."

A grin spread across his face as he licked the coconut cream from his lips. "Hmm that's good. So good, I think you need to taste this pie."

What? Nathan wasn't mad?

With a determined stride, he started for her, and she took a step back. Soon the back of her legs pressed against the cabinet, and she could go no further.

Trapped, he placed his arms on either side of her, and then he kissed her. His mouth moved over hers in a delicious way, smearing the coconut pie across her face.

A giggle erupted from her and yet the move was both sensual and erotic as a tremor of desire spiraled up her spine. With a bang, her heart began to race and her breathing became labored as his hands gripped her head and held her mouth against his.

His tongue delved between her lips, sending tremors like bombs ricocheting through her body. He pressed his body against hers, the hard ridge of him between her legs. A memory of him taking her that night in Vegas slammed into her, and she wrapped her arms around him wanting him closer.

Why did this feel so right? And yet she didn't want forever, but maybe for right now.

The doorbell rang and at first, they ignored the ringing, their mouths melded together. Finally, they pulled apart and stared at one another.

"Someone's at the door," she groaned.

"I can't answer the door," he said. "I have coconut pie all over me and..."

Feeling the hardness between her thighs, she started to laugh. "Go get cleaned up and I'll get the door."

He took her finger and trailed it down his face, collecting pie. Putting the digit in his mouth, he licked her finger, giving the end a little nibble, sending a rush of desire through her. "We might have to try this again."

A smile spread across her face, though she knew she was playing with danger.

They peeled apart, and he went to the bathroom, while she walked to the door. When she swung the door open, shock filled her.

"Congratulations," her sister and Aaron said standing there with Heather and a cake.

𝍠

EXPECTING A DELIVERY, Caitlyn stared at her family stunned. "Hello. You're back," she said reaching out and giving her sister a hug.

"What is in your hair?"

"Coconut Cream pie," she said wondering how she would explain this little accident.

"Come in," she said.

When she hugged Heather, the woman whispered in her ear. "Coconut cream pie? Looks more like whipped cream. What did we interrupt?"

"Nothing," she hissed. "Get your mind out of the gutter."

Funny, if they had been five minutes later, they might not have answered the door at all. If not interrupted she would be spread out on the counter experiencing pie in new areas she never encountered before.

"We came over to say congratulations," Whitney said as she handed her the cake.

"Thank you," Caitlyn said. "As I'm sure you've heard the wedding was not exactly planned."

Why did she think she needed to explain to Whitney? This was between her and Nathan.

"Oh, I knew that as soon as I learned the name of the groom. Speaking of, where is he?"

Nathan walked around the corner, his hair wet, and she

wondered if he'd taken a cold shower. A secretive smile splayed across her face.

"Honey, they brought us a cake to celebrate our wedding."

"Hey guys, did you have fun on your honeymoon," Nathan asked.

"Yes, we did, but it sounds like we missed quite the party after we left. How many tequila shots did you have before you said, 'I do?' "

Caitlyn blushed and realized Aaron was told they drank too much that night. "More than our fair share."

"And we weren't drinking the cheap liquor. Oh, no, we choose to drink the best." Nathan came over and wrapped his arm around her and pulled her to him. "But that night began our journey, and we couldn't be happier."

Whitney stared at Caitlyn, and she wanted the earth to open up and swallow her whole. Neither sister was a dummy, and both knew of Caitlyn's plans. "I'm shocked. For years, you guys have hated each other and Caitlyn you planned on some exotic vacation to meet your Mr. Perfect."

Caitlyn deserved an Academy Award as she gazed at Nathan. "Yes, but it seems Mr. Perfect persuaded me to throw out my dreams and follow him to a wedding chapel on the strip."

"That's not what you said when you came back to the hotel room," Heather said.

"We went for a fake ceremony, but somehow we made it real," she said with a little laugh.

"Would you like to see the video," Nathan said squeezing Caitlyn. "That will answer your questions."

In some ways she hated that record of their ceremony and yet it did make everything clear. For some reason you could hear Caitlyn asking him to make the marriage real. Something she still didn't understand.

"Why is there pie all over the floor and the counter," Heather asked?

Nathan winked at Caitlyn. "Don't ask."

"Oh dear, we interrupted you two love birds," Whitney said her eyes widening.

That wasn't the kind of rumor she needed going around town. As she glanced at the men, Aaron grinned at Nathan like you dog you.

"No, I had come home from the grocery store and the pie fell out of my hands when I was putting it in the refrigerator. That's why it took me so long to come to the door."

Whitney laughed. "Uh huh, why is it in your hair."

Great, just great. If they arrived twenty minutes earlier, they would have seen Amanda the instigator of this mess. Even now, Caitlyn did not like the idea of her kissing her husband. Even if their marriage was only going to be short term, he was hers for the next seventy-five days.

"Let's cut the cake and you guys can tell us all about your honeymoon," Nathan said.

Thank goodness, he was thinking logically. Her sister Heather would be an excellent lawyer, always getting to the truth.

"I'll make some coffee," she said.

"I'll help," Heather replied.

Whitney went into the living area with the men, while her and Heather listened to the three of them whispering and gasping at the video.

Heather stared at her. "Honey, you have cream on your face." She handed her a paper towel. "Here wipe your face off. There's some in your hair."

Oh, no. How did she explain this?

"Honestly, we were arguing, and I threw the pie at him."

Her brows raised. "But how in the world did the cream get all over you?"

Why had she confessed to her sister when she could have remained quiet.

Her cheeks heated. "He chased me down, and we kiss..."

SYLVIA MCDANIEL

"At first, I didn't believe you when you told me you would remain married. I thought there must be something going on here, especially after you returned to the room all upset. But now I'm seeing things between the two of you I didn't expect. Maybe there is something to this Cupid statue business."

The memory of running into Nathan that night slammed into her, and she gasped. She'd forgotten all about how he was the first person she saw that night.

"No," she said. "No, I don't believe in that nonsense."

"Yet, you're living proof of the Cupid Superstition working," Heather said.

Oh, no. That silly superstition was just that and would never work between her and Nathan. Never.

The coffee finished brewing, and they poured the hot liquid into cups. She cut the cake, and they carried it all into the living area.

"Hey, man, I'm sorry to learn your uncle died. The one who did so well in real estate, right?" Aaron asked Nathan.

Stunned, Caitlyn shot a quick glance at her husband.

What?

Why didn't *she* know about his uncle's death?

"Yes, he passed away a week or so before the wedding."

"I remember you saying he was single and had a lot of money. What happened to his estate?" Aaron asked.

"Charity," Nathan said. "He left everything to charity."

Weird, his uncle died right before they made their agreement? Right before she agreed to pretend to be his wife?

"You don't appear drunk in the video," Whitney said. "Mom and Dad are arguing that, if we hadn't gone to Vegas, you wouldn't be in the situation you're in now." She glanced between the two of them and smiled. "From where I'm sitting, it appears to me you two made the right decision. I'm thinking Nathan is good for you, Caitlyn."

Oh, dear God!

Was Caitlyn's acting skills better than she thought?

Were people really buying into their farce so easily?

Aaron grinned. "I believe all that hostility was just to hide the sexual chemistry between you. You know that tension we felt when we walked in the house, like we interrupted something? Your parents are wrong, Whitney; this marriage has a real good chance of making it."

Quickly, Caitlyn shot another glance at Nathan, who was currently wearing a sheepish look on his face. Everyone was starting to believe they were really married in the heart, and not just on paper. Suddenly, she wondered how they would separate their lives now that they'd been joined.

CHAPTER SIXTEEN

$\mathcal{F}$or the first time, Nathan had doubts about their make-believe marriage. If they had not been interrupted tonight, he would have laid her out on the counter. When their friends and family had arrived, the two of them would have been busy doing the wild thing right there in the kitchen for everyone to see.

In fact, the thought of smearing coconut cream pie all over her naked body, then slowly licking it off, was enough to have him ready to race out to the grocery store that very moment.

Unfortunately, all the stores in Cupid rolled up their sidewalks early, or else he probably would've been long gone, buying that pie.

After their guests left, they carried the dirty dishes into the kitchen, where, together, they begin to load the dishwasher. Silent they worked until finally he couldn't stand it any longer. He wanted her to speak to him.

"Tonight was fun."

"Yes," she said. "What are they going to think when we break up?"

That part of this union was something he was beginning to

worry about. At the time, this had all seemed so easy, so simple. but now their family and friends were involved and thought of them as a couple. He always believed they would think Caitlyn, an impetuous woman, had simply made a mistake.

As doubts formed, he wasn't sure what he wanted everyone to think about their union. Especially with the end looming not all that far down the road.

"It's not going to be as easy as I imagined it would be," he admitted.

Hell, he didn't know what to think of their marriage. So far, the experience had been fun and exciting, and had made him realize he did like Caitlyn much more than he ever thought he did before. He thought their time together would be ninety-one days of sparring with one another, not the pleasure her company had instead been.

"No," she said softly. "When Aaron said he would miss our battles tonight, I laughed, because it was kind of funny...until I thought about it. Did we really fight that much?"

Oh, yes. It had been like poking a bear, and in some ways, he enjoyed every moment arguing with her.

"Oh just every single time we saw one another," he said. "You enjoyed constantly reminding me how you possess both beauty *and* brains."

"And you always liked to remind me I was the stupidest woman on the planet."

"No," he replied, confused and wondering what he'd ever said to make her feel that way. "I don't think that at all."

"You don't?"

"No. In fact, I tried to intimidate you, because I believed *you* were smarter than *me*."

A woman's intelligence could be a little intimidating for a man, but most especially for a young kid. Girls were supposed to be the dumber ones, or at least that's what his father had told him. But he didn't see that with Caitlyn

She turned to gaze at him. "Really?"

"Yes," he said, stunned. "You're the girl who outsmarted me in the election. Afterwards, you won the game tournament. Every time I turned around, you outmaneuvered me."

An intelligent and beautiful woman, Caitlyn could make you look stupid in a second.

"That's because I *had* to be better than you, so you wouldn't think I was dumb."

Stepping over to her, he shook his head. "We were adversaries because I wanted to be the smartest kid in class and you always outdid me."

Throughout his school years, he'd strove to outsmart everyone in school, and she'd been the one person he could never outdo.

"What about Amanda?" She asked, changing the direction of the conversation.

"Nothing serious happened between us," he said, knowing for certain Amanda was not meant for him. "Tonight, I forgot all about our dinner date. She was more habit than interest."

"I don't want to be your habit," she said, turning to him, her sapphire eyes flashing with annoyance.

But he didn't want her to just be his habit.

The memory of the coconut pie returned, and he wondered what would have happened if her family hadn't interrupted them.

As he wiped his hands on a towel. The kitchen was now clean. "Good. Want to go play Tomb Raider?"

"Let the games begin!"

CHAPTER SEVENTEEN

*S*itting in the house, Caitlyn glanced around the room and sighed. Today, she took a huge risk. Closer and closer the days moved toward the halfway point, and this afternoon, Caitlyn had put down a deposit on her trip to St. Tropez. The travel agent in Dallas had helped her arrange her reservations, and the final payment was due in two weeks.

Certain she would complete this challenge, she had taken a short-term loan at the bank for the balance of the money, putting her salon up as collateral. It was a risky move, but one she felt confident would pay off in the end. Once she received the check from Nathan anyway.

But what if he didn't compensate her?

Their track record before their marriage was not so good.

Was she placing too much trust in him?

If her parents knew, they would have tried to talk her out of the steps she'd taken, but this just confirmed her commitment to finding Mr. Perfect.

Glancing around at Nathan's home, frustration overwhelmed her, and she didn't understand why.

Had she done the right thing?

Or had she risked everything on a man who had hurt her so deeply in the past?

If he didn't give her the money he'd promised her, she would lose everything.

The clock was ticking, and in little over a month, she would know if the risk had paid off.

The doorbell rang, and she went to the door.

When she swung the door open, a man in a suit stood there with a briefcase. "Is Nathan Greene available?"

"He's not home at the moment. Can I help you?"

"Are you his wife?"

Surprised the man would ask, she gazed at him. "Yes, who are you?"

"I'm Ed Shanker, the attorney handling his uncle's affairs," he explained. "Can I come in?"

"Yes, Nathan should be home any minute. Is he expecting you?"

Why would the lawyer come to Nathan's house instead of meeting him in his own office?

This just seemed odd to her.

After Caitlyn let him in, a disturbing thought suddenly began nagging her, *What if this guy isn't a lawyer at all?*

"Have a seat. Nathan should be home any time. May I get you anything to drink?" she asked him.

"A glass of water would be wonderful, if it's not too much trouble."

When Caitlyn walked into the kitchen, she grabbed her phone from the counter and quickly texted Nathan. "Your uncle's attorney is at the house."

He replied immediately. "Almost there. Keep him occupied."

Though she felt a small amount of relief knowing he was close, she knew she would feel a whole lot better when Nathan actually arrived. She got the lawyer a glass of ice water and took it, and her phone, back into the living room to wait for Nathan.

Caitlyn handed him the water and informed him she'd texted Nathan and confirmed he was nearly there. Then she took a seat on a chair across from where he sat on the couch.

For a moment, they simply stared at one another, and she began to feel an uncomfortable trickle of alarm at the man's perusal. His intent study of her didn't seem sexual by any means, and was more as if he were genuinely interested in knowing everything about her.

"How long have you and Mr. Greene been married?" he asked.

"Not long. Two months and counting," she said. "We were wed in Vegas after my sister's wedding."

The man nodded his head and glanced around at the house.

"When did you meet Nathan?"

Was he simply asking her these questions for small talk, or did he seem a little too interested in her and Nathan's marriage?

Whatever the reason, his questions made her uneasy.

"Well, the first time we ever met would have been in kindergarten. We grew up in Cupid and went to school together."

"A long time then," he said.

"Yes." Wanting to change the subject, she turned the questioning back on him. "Nathan doesn't say much about this uncle. When did he die?"

The man told her the date, and she realized his uncle's passing had occurred only one week before they'd married.

"When was the funeral held?"

"February seventh," he answered.

Stunned, she finally understood why Nathan had been driving home so late on the night their paths crossed back when she'd done the Cupid Stupid Dance. Guilt filled her, causing her heart to ache with regret. He'd been at a family member's funeral earlier that day, and she'd treated him horribly that very same night.

Just as she'd been treating him so badly since that silly

campaign they'd run against each other in junior high. Looking back now, the whole childish event seemed immature and stupid. Neither one had wanted to be the first to give in and simply forgive the other over all these years.

And it made her feel ashamed to realize it had been Nathan who had taken the first step toward forgiveness by burying the hatchet and even going so far as to marry her, legitimately or not.

"Our wedding was exactly a week later," she told him, and for the first time, Caitlyn came to the realization they had said I do at midnight on Valentine's Day.

The date had never meant much to her before, but suddenly, that day seemed important.

But why?

Their marriage would end as soon as he received the contract and the ninety-one days were over. On May fifteenth, she would once again be a free woman.

With a sigh, she realized getting out of this union was not going to be as easy or as painless as she'd once imagined. But she knew she couldn't back out now, or she would lose everything.

She decided her life would likely be much simpler if she didn't take on so many challenges, dares and gambles.

The whir of the garage door signaled Nathan had arrived home and relief overwhelmed her. Now, *he* could talk to this attorney.

"He's home!" she announced unnecessarily, then sprang up and ran to the back door.

When Nathan walked in, a sense of comfort filled her. Why, she didn't know, but she didn't understand why the lawyer was here.

"Honey, your uncle's lawyer is in the living room," she said loud enough the other man could hear them, then gave Nathan a quick kiss on the lips before taking his briefcase from his hands.

Nathan smiled at her and gave her a hug.

"Thanks for keeping him entertained," he whispered in her ear.

He gently held her face in his hands, pressing his lips just above her brow before releasing her, and she watched him go as he left the kitchen.

"Good to see you, Ed," Nathan said. "Let's go into my office, and we can discuss what you came to see me about."

Stunned he would take the man somewhere she couldn't listen in, Caitlyn frowned.

Was he hiding something from her?

If so, what?

"Great," the man said, rising and following Nathan into the room, where he closed the door behind them.

As she watched them disappear, a trickle of anger spiraled down her spine.

What were they keeping so damned secret?

An image of the travel brochure popped into her mind as the wave of anger began to grow, and she could admit to herself there was a whole lot of hurt mixed in to that anger as well. She decided she was glad she had gone ahead and taken the chance on booking her vacation to find her Mr. Perfect.

She decided Nathan *would* pay her, or she'd hire an attorney of her own to get the money he owed her, and maybe even more, just to show him she wasn't one to be messed with.

If he could have secrets, well, so could she.

CHAPTER EIGHTEEN

*N*athan walked the attorney to the door, where they said their goodbyes. The other man's entire visit had been a test to verify they legitimately lived together as a married couple, and thanks to Caitlyn, they'd passed. On day ninety-one, the money would be transferred into his account.

At that moment, on the inside, he was dancing. So far, everything was going exactly as planned.

After he showed the man out the door, he walked into the kitchen where Caitlyn was cooking them dinner. One thing he loved about her being here, was her willingness to take over the cooking. There'd been far less takeout since she moved in.

"Thanks for visiting with him until I got home."

Without a word, she only shrugged, and an icy chill filled the room.

Oh hell, what had he done now?

Walking up behind her, he placed his hands on her shoulders, rubbing them gently, while she stirred a pot containing something which smelled delicious.

"What are you hiding?" she asked suddenly, surprising him with the bite in her tone and the question itself.

SYLVIA MCDANIEL

"Huh? What are you talking about?"

"You took him into your office so I couldn't hear what you two discussed. Were you arranging the annulment with him?"

"What? No," he said, stunned she would think he would already have the paperwork done. Nothing could be processed until after the ninety-one days.

Was that why she was so tense and angry?

Didn't she *want* the annulment, so she could find her rich husband?

"I took him in the office so we could discuss the final affairs of my uncle. His visit concerned my uncle's will and there was some paperwork for me to sign. I just figured the office would be more appropriate. I didn't mean to make you feel as if you weren't allowed to be there. I guess I just assumed you wouldn't have found it very interesting."

It sounded like a perfectly plausible explanation to him, but would she accept his reasoning?

What he and the attorney had spoken about was not something he wanted her to know the details of, and she certainly couldn't learn the real reason for their marriage. When–*if*– he ever found a woman to have a real marriage with, he wanted to know she loved him for him, and not his money. But when it came to Caitlyn, she'd already made it perfectly clear it was all about the money for her.

And in a way, he could appreciate the fact she was honest about it. Most women would deny and hide their true intentions. Not her though.

"Mr. Shanker is busy closing out my uncle's affairs. It's sad when someone dies and the only family they have left are nieces and nephews. My uncle never married nor had any children of his own."

Finally, she turned in his arms and gazed up at him. Pressing her chest against him, she finally relaxed. Oh, God, holding her this way felt so good. *Too* good.

"That is sad, but at least he did have you and the rest of your family. Are you the executor then?"

"Oh, no, but he left me some stocks and bonds, so I had to sign for the transfer."

He wasn't lying; his uncle *had* left him those things. He just wasn't telling her everything, which was these particular stocks and bonds were worth millions. And with his uncle's properties, Nathan's future wealth would be well over a billion dollars. Some of which he would share with his family, just because he thought there was plenty of money and it seemed as if it were the right thing to do.

But the majority of that money would only come to him if he and Caitlyn remained married for the full ninety-one days, as his uncle had wished.

"While I know my feelings may sound crazy, it seemed as if you were hiding something from me. Sometimes I need to remind myself this isn't a real marriage."

Sometimes *he* wanted it to never end.

He grinned at her. "So if we were a true husband and wife, you would have insisted on being in there with me?"

"Yes, I don't want secrets in my real marriage. Even though my plan is to marry a wealthy man, he'll know this from the beginning, but he'll also know I will be his wife in every way, and that he can always trust me. After all, if you can't trust the person you're married to, why get married at all?"

Her words stung. Their union was real in the legal sense, just not one that would last forever, and yet things between them were satisfying in a way he had never planned.

These last two months had brought them closer together, and the dynamics of their relationship was different. But he needed to keep reminding himself she didn't believe he was enough for her. Therefore, this union would end on day ninety-one, without question.

"Agree, but our marriage is not going to last," he said.

Once again, she tensed in his arms.

Did she want them to stay married?

Why was she tensing and getting upset?

"We agreed to ninety-one days," he reminded her.

"Yes, but it sounds so heinous when you say we're not going to last. Yes, I've known from the start this is only for a short length of time, but I never expected to feel like a failure. You know I hate losing. My competitive, winning nature is something I'm dealing with on a daily-basis here."

For them to each continue with their lives, they would have to separate then either obtain a divorce, or an annulment, but she had accepted this from the beginning.

The doorbell rang, and they sighed.

"Now who?" he grumbled.

Wanting some alone time with his wife, he went to the door expecting to shoo whoever it was away. But when he opened the portal, Caitlyn's mother strolled right on through, passing him by as if he didn't even exist.

"Caitlyn, your father is impossible!" she cried out upon finding her daughter in the kitchen.

"Yes, Mother, I'm aware. What has he done now?"

"Where should I begin?" she said, removing her coat and glancing around the kitchen. "Nice house."

"Thank you," Nathan said, taking her jacket. "Great to see you, Mrs. Beckett, or should I call you mother?"

The woman turned to glare at him, and he could see he had gotten to her. "Call me Louise," she practically snarled.

A smile crossed his face. There was something he hadn't thought through when he'd married Caitlyn: not only had he married her, but he'd married her family as well.

He wondered how they would take the inevitable divorce or annulment. Probably not any better than they took the surprise marriage.

"Would you like to have dinner with us?" he asked, doing his best to appeal to her nicer side.

"Of course, why do you think I'm here?" she questioned, her tone making it clear he should have known this. "Of all my girls, Caitlyn's the best cook, and I am certainly not about to eat with Milton tonight."

What an interesting turn of events. His mother- and father-in-law were having problems, and he wondered if they had these types of disagreements often.

Reaching up into the cabinet, he pulled down enough table settings for three.

"Your father is impossibly tight with our money. So tight, I swore to him I'm going to divide our assets."

Caitlyn turned and stared. "What did he say?"

Her mother gave an evil laugh. "Milton told me over his dead body, and I told *him* that could be arranged."

"You didn't!" Caitlyn exclaimed in shock, though her face broke out into an amused grin.

"I did. And that's when he ordered me to get out." Louise sighed. "So I packed my suitcase and I'm moving in with you."

Nathan jerked around from the refrigerator, his heart skipping more than a few beats, and stared at Caitlyn, who had spun from the stove to stare at her mother at nearly the same time.

Dear God, his mother-in-law was going to *live* with them?

How was this going to work?

He and Caitlyn would always have to be on their guard.

Oh, why couldn't one of Caitlyn's sisters have been the better cook!

CHAPTER NINETEEN

*T*he luscious dinner Caitlyn had fixed tasted like cardboard to her. All she could think about was how to sneak her things from the guest bedroom to Nathan's, without her mother knowing.

Also, how was she going to be able to get any sleep lying beside Nathan, for as long as it took until her mother and father decided to reconcile?

What if they never did!

Surely this was just a bump in the road, and they would soon be back together. Sure, her father could be a complete horse's ass, but the thought of her parents getting a divorce caused her stomach to reel.

She gave up pretending to eat and pushed her plate aside.

"Mom, why don't you clean the kitchen while Nathan and I prepare the guest room?" she suggested, and saw her husband's eyes widen.

"No, there's no need to straighten the room. As long as I have a bed, I'm fine."

Her chest tightened and she glanced at her husband.

"We understand, but the bed needs to be unloaded of all my

stuff. When I moved in, we just threw my things in there, thinking we had time to sort through it all later," Caitlyn explained, wishing her mother would simply accept her explanation and cooperate for once.

"Let me help you," her mother said.

"By cleaning the kitchen, you will be," Caitlyn promised. "It won't take Nathan and me but a minute to straighten the guest room."

Caitlyn and Nathan pushed their chairs back from the table, stood, and rushed towards the stairs, not allowing her mother time to further thwart their plans. Not only did they need a moment alone to talk, but she had to move all her things before her mother realized where she'd been sleeping.

"What is happening right now?" Nathan asked, a panicked expression on his face, which probably matched Caitlyn's perfectly. "Your mother is going to live with us?"

"What do you want me to do, throw her out? My parents have never separated before. "

"Why can't she stay in your apartment?"

They had just reached the top of the stairs when he asked that question, which caused her to freeze in her tracks and stare at him. "And just how do I explain the reason I'm keeping my apartment?"

He growled with frustration.

"Can I just say your family is weird as hell?" he said.

"You're telling me. I've been living with them for over twenty-five years. I *know* how weird they are."

When they reached her room, she stood in the doorway and shook her head, glancing around at the private sanctuary she was being forced to relinquish. This room had become her place to escape each time she felt tempted around her husband, or when she just needed somewhere to be alone in order to put everything back in perspective.

"What are we going to do?" he asked.

She could tell he felt as defeated as she did, but they both also knew they could do anything if they worked as a team.

"It appears I'm moving into your room. Unless you'd rather I come clean with her and tell her the truth."

"No, you're sleeping in my room," he said, grinning wide. "Where do we begin?"

"First, you're going to agree there will be no hanky-panky, slap and tickle, or anything else sexual."

"You're no fun," he pouted playfully. "So we're supposed to sleep together, but not touch one another?"

"That's right," she said, looking around the room. "You grab all my clothes out of the closet, and I'll carry my toiletries from the bathroom."

"I'm going to see you naked," he taunted.

"You've already seen me naked," she responded. Stopping and staring at him, she grimaced. "Do you think this is a joke? My parents' marriage is imploding, and I have to sleep with you for the rest of our time, or Mother goes home, whichever comes first."

"Maybe I need to thank your mother," he teased.

Why did she feel as if he was enjoying every minute of this fiasco?

Together, they hauled her stuff into his bedroom in no time at all.

When Caitlyn's eyes fell upon his bed, she knew she would dread that night, and every night thereafter, for the time her mother stayed with them.

"Do you have an extra set of sheets for that bed?"

"Of course," he said, and grabbed them from the hall closet.

The two of them made the bed she'd been sleeping in ever since the day she'd moved in two months ago.

With a sigh, they pulled up the comforter and stood, both simply staring at the bed. Until her mother left, this would be a test of their commitment to this scheme of his.

Could they continue to make her mother believe they were truly a married couple?

Or would their deception be discovered and everything they'd worked so hard for all be for naught?

Glancing around the room, she looked for any other evidence which would show she had been sleeping in the guest room.

"Did we get everything?"

"I think so," he said. "Hot times tonight."

"Cool your jets. Not with your mother-in-law two doors down."

A frown crossed his face. "How long is this going to last?"

"Do you think I know?" she asked. "Why don't you go bring up her suitcases from the car, while I call my sisters and tell them what's going on?"

Shaking his head, he went down the stairs as Caitlyn pulled out her phone and quickly called Heather. But her call went straight to voicemail.

Caitlyn remembered Heather had her study group on that night, so she probably wasn't taking any calls at the moment. She tried Whitney next, and when she answered, loud music and people talking and laughing echoed back through the phone.

"What's up, sis? We're out with some of Aaron's friends. Can I call you back?"

"Did you know our parents are separated?"

"What did you say?"

Stepping into Nathan's bathroom, she raised her voice as loud as she dared without her mother hearing. "Family emergency. Our parents are separated!"

Why had her mother chosen *her* home to escape from her marriage?

Her sister was silent, but the background noise remained. "Hold on," she finally said to Caitlyn, then to someone else, said, "I'll be right back."

The noise faded more and more, until at last, it was much quieter and only the faint muted sound of music could be heard.

"Sorry, I had to walk outside." Whitney laughed and said, "For a moment there, I thought you said our parents had separated. Isn't that hilarious! So what was it you really said?"

"That *is* what I really said! Our parents *are* separated, and for some reason, Mother chose to come here and move in with me and Nathan while she and Dad are split up."

Tears welled up in Caitlyn's eyes. Everyone knew her father was difficult to live with, but her mother was no walk in the park either.

What had finally driven the two of them apart?

Sure, her father was a tightwad and her mother liked to shop, but they had dealt with that very problem for years.

Often, they argued over their children, but didn't most parents?

And then a horrible thought crossed her mind.

Could her father be having an affair?

With the way her father believed marriage was forever, it couldn't possibly be that.

Could it?

"No, I don't believe this," Whitney said. "Aaron and I will be right over. They've been arguing, but they always argue."

"Do you think he's having an affair?"

"*What*! No! Well, I don't know, but give me thirty minutes, and we'll get to the bottom of this."

"Pick up Heather from her study group and bring her too," Caitlyn said. "I'm texting her now."

"See you soon," Whitney said shortly, before disconnecting the call.

Yes, Nathan was right. Without a doubt, her family was absolutely weird. She'd even amp it up a bit to say they were all batshit crazy.

Just then, Heather responded to her text. "WTF?"

CHAPTER TWENTY

*T*hese people weren't simply weird, as he'd thought earlier; now he was leaning more towards they were crazy as hell. Probably certifiable!

Nathan had just taken his mother-in-law's luggage to the guest room when the doorbell rang as he was coming back downstairs. Caitlyn was upstairs with her mother, trying to settle her in, so he swung the door open and her two sisters and Aaron rushed inside.

"Where is she!" Whitney bellowed.

Heather stood off to the side, leaning against the wall, her arms crossed and brows raised, and a look of amusement on her face. "Boys, welcome to the family, where crazy runs rampant."

Aaron laughed, but Nathan only raised his own brows.

Whitney called up the stairs, a frantic tone to her voice. "Caitlyn, Mom? Are you guys up there?"

The two women came hurrying down.

Louise looked at Whitney. "Darling, what are you doing here? And Heather too? Did someone call a family meeting?"

What did she think was going to happen once she told Caitlyn she'd left her husband?

"Yes, *I* did," Caitlyn said. "Let's all go into the living room and sit down so you can tell us what's going on."

Nathan watched as his wife herded her relatives into their family space. His own parents had died when he and his siblings were quite young , and his younger brother was currently in the military and his sister attended college in New York, so he didn't have a lot of experience in this department.

Once a month, they spoke by phone, but they didn't have a relationship like this. And their parents had never separated.

Once everyone was seated, Mrs. Beckett smiled at her children. "Divorce happens in a lot of families. Your father gave me grief one too many times, and when he told me to get out, I decided I'd had enough. So I packed my bags and left."

Now he understood where Caitlyn received her drama gene: her mother. The two women were so much alike.

"Daddy would never tell you to leave," Heather responded. "He's difficult, but he's not stupid, and he knows you make his life easier in the long run."

A true statement. But sometimes men didn't realize how their wives made their life more pleasant. At least, Nathan hadn't, until Caitlyn came along.

"Probably, a little too easy," their mother said. "Personally, I think he meant for me to leave the room because we couldn't come to an agreement. Very seldom do I put my foot down, but this time, I did. And when he said get out, I decided the time was right for me to do exactly that and go."

Silence filled the room.

"Does he realize you've left?"

"Milton's city council meeting is tonight, so he'll find out a little after nine o'clock I'm missing."

Her mother appeared so cool and reserved and totally in control. If she had been playing a game of chess, she would've just called out checkmate.

Would their father come pounding on the door sometime tonight as well?

"Before the entire city law enforcement goes out searching for you, did you happen to think to leave him a note or something, telling him where you are?" Whitney asked.

A smile crossed Louise's face, and Nathan was overcome by the oddest feeling. His home was going to end up being ground zero for this war between husband and wife.

"Yes, I did. And I also told him I was not speaking to him. If he wanted to talk to me, he would need to speak to our daughters. I'm only talking to my girls."

From the sounds of it, this battle was not going to end anytime soon.

"What were you arguing about?" Heather, always the practical one, asked.

"Money," she said. "Your father and I have enough to last us a lifetime, unless something drastic happens, but you'd think we were misers, and I'm tired of him being so stingy."

Maybe this was the reason Caitlyn was so intent on marrying a billionaire. After listening to her parents argue for so long about funds, she likely didn't want her own marriage to be the same.

Nathan decided he needed to dig a little deeper into her reasons for wanting to marry a rich man.

Could her family arguments have made her fearful of being broke?

"Mom, the two of you should see a counselor," Whitney advised. "Someone to help you talk through your problems."

His mother-in-law laughed out loud at that idea. "Do you think your father would talk to someone who might tell him he was wrong?"

The three daughters grew silent.

"If he thought you weren't coming back, he might," Heather said, a look of thoughtful deviousness upon her face. "I should draw up a separation agreement. That way, he'll believe you're serious."

Stunned, Nathan realized for the first time that evening his mother-in-law would be with them for a while. That could be both good *and* bad. Good for him to be able to share a bed with his wife, but bad–so very, *unbelievably bad*–if she learned the truth about their marriage.

Louise turned and stared at Heather. "Who said I wasn't serious? A divorce would give me enough money to live my life the way I want to and happily. No more fighting. No more dragging him to places I want to go and listening to him bitch. You girls are grown. We should be having fun in our lives at this point."

"You've thought this through, haven't you?" Caitlyn asked. "How long has this been brewing?"

Mentally, Nathan groaned. No longer would his peaceful house be the quiet sanctuary he imagined it would always be.

And it was certainly not one where he could seduce his wife.

"Since you were a child," she said.

"Is he having an affair?" Caitlyn blurted.

Her mother started laughing. "The man doesn't know the first thing about romance. Who would have him? He wouldn't know how to date or attract or even how to *find* a woman."

"Are *you* having an affair, Mother?" Heather asked.

"No, but if I found the right man, you damn well better believe I would in a heartbeat." Her eyes widened suddenly. "I'll do what Caitlyn had planned to do. I'll fly to St. Tropez and find me a rich younger man!"

The three girls gazed at each other in horror. It was all Nathan could do to keep from busting out laughing. The three sisters had just received the shock of their life, thinking about their mother with another man, and a young one at that!

"*Mother!*" Caitlyn cried out in admonishment.

Louise turned and glared at her sons-in-law. "I'm warning you two; make my daughters happy, and if you can't, then move over and let another man please them."

How was Nathan to respond to *that*?

So he looked to Aaron, who was smiling at their mother-in-law. "Don't worry, Whitney and I are blessed."

She glanced over at Nathan, and he stared at Caitlyn, who was giving him a pleading look. "Not a problem, Mrs. Beckett. Caitlyn and I are still on our honeymoon, and we don't plan on ever leaving it."

What was he saying?

Their marriage was a lie. But no matter what, he *did* want Caitlyn to be happy, and tonight he'd gained a deeper understanding of her and where she came from.

How had his own upbringing affected his ideas of happily ever after?

As far as he knew and could remember, his mother and father had loved each other deeply.

Just then, Whitney's phone rang, and they all stared at the device. "It's Daddy."

"Well? Answer it," her mother commanded. "But don't tell him where I'm at."

They heard his voice clearly without him even being on speaker. "Where the hell is your mother!"

"Go to bed, Daddy. Get some rest, and tomorrow, you might want to google how to show your wife you love her." And with that, Whitney disconnected the call.

Never a dull moment in this family he married into, Nathan thought. Maybe being a short-term member wasn't such a bad thing.

"Aaron, time to take me home," Whitney said.

"Me too," Heather responded. "Try to sleep, Mother. Everything will look better in the morning."

She gave each of her daughters a hug goodbye, then assured them, saying, "No matter what happens, I'm going to be all right."

Once the door shut behind the others, she turned to Caitlyn and Nathan. "Goodnight, dears. Being newlyweds, I'm sure you're ready for me to disappear."

Nathan knew tonight would be awkward for him and Caitlyn. Just when they were beginning to feel comfortable with one another, life had thrown him a mother-in-law situation.

CHAPTER TWENTY-ONE

*C*aitlyn undressed in the bathroom, but she couldn't hide in there forever. Nathan was already in bed.

How were they going to cope with this situation with her mother?

How would she exit this marriage without creating her own drama and mess?

Finally, she turned off the light and walked out into the bedroom. He was sitting, reading a magazine for gamers.

She crawled onto the other side and pulled the covers up to her chest. The urge to place a bedroll between them was tempting, but they'd already had sex once. If he wanted her, the only thing stopping him was his conscience.

"Goodnight," she said, then rolled away from him.

"Goodnight." The man continued reading his magazine, not touching her, and she breathed a sigh of relief.

When her head hit the pillow, her mind went into overdrive. Her parents could be getting a divorce. Her family was coming apart at the seams, and the tension from tonight suddenly overwhelmed her. Moisture sprang into her eyes.

Oh, God, she didn't want to cry. But the sadness, and the way her mother was handling the situation, overcame her. Tears rolled down her cheeks, and she tried not to sniff, but failed.

Nathan turned the light out, keeping to his side of the bed.

She sniffed again, and then a little sob snuck out when she'd been trying so hard to be quiet.

"Are you crying?"

"No," she lied, not wanting his sympathy, and not wanting to admit how much this situation upset her.

Tears streamed down her face now, and she sniffed several times.

"You're lying," he admonished, then rolled over and took her in his arms.

At his touch, the water works unleashed in a storm of ragged emotion.

Holding her in his embrace, he tried to soothe her. "Don't cry. Lots of parents divorce."

"Not mine," she said with a hiccup. "And she didn't say what fight brought about the breakup. Heather told me they fought over what she paid for Whitney's wedding gown. What if they were fighting about us this time?"

That was her biggest fear, that somehow, she had caused this strife between her parents. Whatever had really sent her mother over the edge, she was being very cagey about the exact details of the argument.

As he held her, he patted her on the back, holding her close to him. "We can't control what they argue about. It sounds like this situation has been coming for quite some time. Your mother is simply not happy."

It was true, and her mother had always been the gatekeeper between her father and his daughters as well. "He's always been unhappy with us. Heather is the only one he's not fought with about something."

Her husband rocked her gently in his arms and a soothing sense of contentment slowly seeped into her bones.

"Do you think it's up to you to make either one of them happy?" he asked. "No, so don't let this upset you. They will find a way to work their problems out, or they will go to court. Either way, in the end, it will work out how it's supposed to."

With a deep steadying breath, she wanted to know more about his own family situation. "I kind of remember your mom and dad. Were they happy?"

"Yes. Right up until the day my father had his heart attack. After that, my mother slowly slipped away," he said. " I still miss them."

While her home had always been a place she loved and felt loved in returned, sometimes the lid seemed to blow off and her father created a row.

Were all families this way, or just hers?

Laying her head against his chest, she nodded. "Mother can be a little obnoxious sometimes, but I understand what she's saying about Daddy. My father can be unyielding and cold."

As long as her father got his way, everything was fine, but buck his system, and the crazy train went off the rails.

"Yes, I can see that. Who knew our first crisis as a married couple would be your family?"

"When we separate, you get to escape from the drama," she said, with a halfhearted laugh.

"Unless your mother is still living with us, and won't leave when you do," he teased.

"How are we going to do this with her here?"

As he squeezed her tightly against him, he whispered in the darkness, "Day by day. We just have to see what happens, day by day, and deal with the results."

They sat there in silence, with him holding her in his arms, comforting her, each lost in their own thoughts. With her mother living here, this was not going to make their supposed marriage simple. If anything, her presence would strain the peace and make them even more nervous.

Part of Caitlyn was disappointed, as she had been enjoying this time with Nathan, but now, she had to share this space with her mother and all the family drama which will come with her.

"Why do you want to marry a billionaire?" he asked. "Could your dreams have anything to do with the fact your father is so tight with the money?"

Stunned, she thought a moment.

Was that the reason she wanted a rich man for a husband?

Always she thought it was because she simply wanted an easier life. Someone who could give her the things she thought she wanted. Someone to protect her from going broke.

With a sudden realization, she realized her mother had constantly instilled in them as children to marry a man with money, rather than someone for love. The memory of her saying it's just as easy to fall in love with a rich man, as a poor one filled Caitlyn's mind.

Caitlyn had taken that message to heart. The memories of her parents struggling surged through her, and she understood she didn't want to live with that fear.

"My father can squeeze a dime out of a turnip. He's been a tightwad all my life, and I grew up with him complaining about any money my mother had spent. Maybe a small part of me doesn't want that kind of life any longer. Mainly, I want my life and my children to be worry free."

Never had she considered how her father's words and attitude had affected her as a child. Yet Nathan had realized quite quickly why she wanted a rich man.

While he held her, he rubbed her back through her night-gown, and her breasts tingled where they were crushed against his chest. Although his hardened manhood rested against her, he wasn't being sexually aggressive, but rather comforting.

112

Comforting, as in she liked the feel of his arms holding her and being here beside him, as if she truly belonged here.

"Are you all right?"

"Yes," she said. "I think I can go to sleep now."

"Okay. I'm not going to hear you sobbing again, am I?"

"No, I'm sorry. I think the emotions of tonight overwhelmed me when I laid down to relax."

"Don't apologize. This has been a rather strange evening."

She laughed. "Are you saying my family is crazy?"

"I would never say those words to your face," he said. Giving her one last squeeze, he kissed the top of her head. "Goodnight, Caitlyn. Get some rest. We're going to need patience over the next few days."

CHAPTER TWENTY-TWO

*T*hree days later, Caitlyn stormed into the house, slamming the door behind her, and wanting to strangle the life out of her mother. "*Mother!*"

Since her mother had moved in with them, Nathan and Caitlyn now greeted each other lovingly when they came home from work. So Nathan walked around the corner with a smile on his face, and said, "Honey, I'm so glad you're home!"

"I'm not in the best moods right now," she warned. "My mother put a wedding announcement in the paper. Everyone in town knows we're married!"

"Shit," he said. "Your family sure doesn't know how to keep secrets."

"You're home, dear," her mother said coming down the steps. "Did you cut a lot of hair today?"

Why did she always demean Caitlyn's salon?

Beauty and Brains was so much more than just a hair salon. It was a place where women could receive a full beauty treatment such as everything from a manicure to a massage, to even facials!

"No, I did not," she said through gritted teeth. "One of my

clients congratulated me on getting married. Did you put an announcement in the paper?"

"Of course! You're my daughter and I wanted everyone to know you and Nathan have wed," she smiled. "Your old childhood enemy."

Nathan grimaced, and so did Caitlyn. They had tried so hard to keep this quiet, in order to limit the drama when they split, and now the whole town likely knew they were married.

Would her mother put their divorce in the paper as well?

"Thank you, but I wish you had spoken to me before you decided to make the announcement," she said.

Now, she'd not only have to contend with all the well-wishes, but what would her clients say when they learned of the separation?

No one expected it to last.

"You're my daughter. Why would I ask you? If you had a proper wedding, we would have announced your engagement, and your bridal picture would have been in the paper. But since you went for a quickie ceremony in Vegas, the least we could do was put something in the paper."

With a sigh, Caitlyn closed her eyes. The deed was done, and she was getting nowhere with her mother. Nothing she could do about it now.

In years to come, what would her children think when they looked back, and she was married once before to her arch enemy?

Nathan didn't say anything, but from the expression on his face, she knew he wasn't pleased. There would be no quiet annulment or divorce as they had wanted. No, thanks to her family, their parting ways would be very public.

"Oh, by the way, your father is on his way," she said. " He received the separation letter today and wants to talk."

Wonderful, her angry father was on his way over here to

discuss–otherwise known as argue–over what her mother was doing. "Do I need to call the sheriff?"

With a jerk, Nathan stared at her, but her mother laughed.

"No, dear, I'm sure he'll do nothing more than his usual ranting and raving about how I'm spending all his money."

What happened to her peaceful environment, where she came home and rested, relaxed, and even played video games with Nathan?

"Is the rest of the family coming over?"

"Only Heather, to advise him on his legal rights," she said. "He'll listen to her."

Of course he would. Heather was the favored one. The intelligent daughter, who was going to law school. Who took after him. His other girls were dingbats, who took after their mother.

"Great," she said. "Another happy night here in our home with my husband and crazy family."

With a laugh her mother headed for the stairs. "I've got to get ready."

After she was gone, Nathan walked over and took Caitlyn in his arms. His lips came down on hers for a quick kiss, almost as if he was trying to instill strength into her.

Why did he feel like a safe haven away from the craziness which was her life?

Why was he and his home the place of comfort she wanted to shelter in?

"Would you like to escape?"

With a laugh, she laid her head on his shoulder. "Right now, I would love to say yes to that idea."

"There's a gaming tournament this weekend in Dallas."

"Really?"

"All day Saturday and part of Sunday," he said. "We can leave either Friday night or Saturday morning; your choice."

"It's a date," she said, thinking she deserved this time off. Her salon was open six days a week, but she never worked week-ends. Only her technicians and other stylists did.

The doorbell rang, and with one last squeeze, she slipped out of his arms and went to the answer the summons. When she opened the door, Heather walked in.

"Hi, Nathan. Wipe your mouth, you're wearing my sister's lipstick."

A grin spread across her husband's face, and for some reason, a sense of satisfaction filled Caitlyn. It was almost as if that lipstick branded him as hers, and yet he would never belong to her.

Legally, yes, but his heart and soul were still up for grabs, and she didn't like that thought.

In fact, she couldn't think about that right now. At the moment, thinking of him with other women was more than she could handle.

The doorbell rang again, and her father strolled through the door when she opened it.

Let the games begin!

"Caitlyn. I can't believe you're letting your mother stay here," her father scolded her.

This was her fault?

It was *her* problem her mother and father couldn't get along?

"What did you want me to do, Daddy, let her sleep on the streets? I can't believe my parents' marriage is falling apart."

His brows drew together in a scowl. "That's nonsense. I'm here to take your mother home."

"Then I hope you came prepared to compromise, because she's pretty determined, and she's not backing down," Caitlyn said.

"Nathan," the older man said as way of a greeting. "Still married to my daughter?"

Caitlyn's ire sparked like the lighting of dynamite as her

stomach clenched. Leave it to her father to say the most irritating comments.

"Yes, sir, Caitlyn and I are doing quite well," he said, pulling her into his arms. "I'd say better than you and Mrs. Beckett."

She had to bite her lip to keep from giggling, and Heather choked on her drink. Sputtering and trying to cough up the liquid she'd been drinking, her sister turned her back and Caitlyn knew she was laughing.

"Well, we've got a lot more traction and garbage accumulated over the years."

"Yes, I'm sure you do," Nathan replied.

Just then, her mother descended the stairs regally, much as a queen would to speak to her subjects. Moving faster than he had in years, her father hurried over to the bottom of the steps.

"Louise, what *are* you doing?"

"I'm wonderful, Milton! How are you this fine evening?"

"But...I didn't ask how you were..."

"Yes, but it's common courtesy, and something you seem to be lacking."

The man stiffened, and Caitlyn realized this was going to be an interesting evening. She pulled Nathan along behind her as she scrambled for a seat on the couch next to her sister. Watching her parents duke it out, literally, in their living room was entertainment they couldn't miss!

"Shall we sit down and talk?" Heather, ever the voice of reason, asked.

Caitlyn wanted to elbow her right in the mouth. It had just started getting good!

Without giving her husband a kiss, or a hug, or anything, her mother strolled over to the chair and sat down–regally, of course–forcing her husband to sit on the couch with his daughters and son-in-law.

"Why did you leave me?" he asked, before his butt had even touched the material of the sofa.

"That's a silly question. You know perfectly well *why*."

"We bought Whitney's wedding dress. And now you want more money?"

"Most parents pay for their daughters' entire weddings. Whitney and Aaron paid for everything but the dress. I insisted she let me buy her wedding gown, and then had to fight your stubborn ass for even that!"

A growl escaped her father. "Well, she should have chosen a cheaper one."

"How much do you think a gown cost these days?"

Oh, she had just set him up; the poor man didn't know the price of a formal dress any more than he knew the price of a regular church dress. The man was about to get slam-dunked and didn't even realize it.

"A couple of hundred dollars," he said, confidently.

With a coy look, her mother took out her phone. The woman had obviously come prepared in advance for this question. "The *average* wedding dress is over one thousand dollars, and if you purchase a designer gown–which we didn't–you can easily double or triple that cost."

Mission accomplished, she closed her phone. "Whitney's elegant and beautiful dress? We paid only eight hundred dollars for her to look so beautiful and glamorous on her wedding day."

"All right, I'll quit complaining. Just come home."

Right now, everyone knew he was only saying whatever she wanted to hear, just so she would come back to him.

"No, Milton. There are going to be some changes in our home if I'm to go back. When was the last time you took me on a date? When was the last time you spent quality time with me doing something *I* loved, without complaining? When was the last time we went on a vacation together?"

Oh dear, her mother was laying out the demands.

Her father's head dropped back, and he shook it, while groaning. "As the mayor of this city, I'm a busy man and don't have time to go on a luxury trip with you."

Already, Caitlyn could see her mother stiffening. "You are so right, Milton. You are a dedicated servant to this fine city. A fine mayor, but a *horrible* husband and a *terrible* father. Enjoy spending your last days on this earth alone."

Like Queen Elizabeth herself, she stood and damn near floated toward the stairs. Her husband jumped up to run after her.

"Louise, wait. Don't go! I didn't mean it that way."

Without looking back or hesitating, Louise climbed the stairs, leaving him at the bottom to stare up at her. As he turned around, her father looked as if he were ready to cry at any moment.

Caitlyn, Heather and Nathan, all sitting frozen on the couch, stared open-mouthed at each other, shocked over the reaction of the man before them.

"Girls, help me," he said, his face stricken. "I don't think she's ever coming home."

CHAPTER TWENTY-THREE

*W*hen they crawled into bed that night, Caitlyn tossed and turned, until finally, Nathan rolled over and took her in his arms. He liked having her in bed with him. He enjoyed the touch of her body snuggled against his.

In the king-size bed, there was plenty of distance between them, but he enjoyed having her close. Each night, once she fell asleep, he sought her out in the big bed.

"They need to figure this out themselves. You can't do it."

"But it's hard seeing my parents fight."

"Your father is no match for your mother. She literally has pinned him up against the wall, with nowhere to turn."

No wonder Caitlyn was such a strategist; she'd learned from observing her mother. Now he understood, when they were kids, how in a very smart way, his slogan was turned against him.

Watching her parents helped him understand her even more.

"How did your parents argue?" she asked, her derriere butting against his growing penis, and he wanted to groan.

Did she have any idea what she did to him?

Did she realize just the touch of her silky flesh against his own was like a match striking an inferno?

How he longed to roll her over and show her the magic they created in Vegas, but knew it would not be a wise move. There were still a few more weeks to go.

"The house became almost deadly silent when my parents fought. One of them would grow angry, and they didn't speak for days. Like a Cold War, they waited to see who could freeze the other one out. Then there would be a heated exchange of them talking before they worked things out."

In the darkness, their breath sounded harsh, almost raspy.

"I'm sorry about the newspaper," she said. "Did you notice she said your childhood enemy? I think she put that in the paper."

Laughter rumbled from his chest. "Well, we *were* childhood enemies."

"Not always. I had a crush on you in elementary school, you know. Even in junior high, right up until that disastrous student council president race."

So their attraction started long before now. Though he didn't want to admit it, he'd always been attracted her as well. If he hadn't botched the student council runoff, who knows what would have happened between them.

"Sometimes things are delayed for a reason," he said, trying to think rationally, but really just wanting to roll on top of her and do what normal married couples do.

Didn't she feel him?

Didn't she understand how much he wanted her?

"I've always wondered why you decided to make me sound so stupid in that race?" she asked softly.

"No, Caitlyn, I wasn't going after you in any way. The gamers wanted me to make my campaign about having the brains to get the job done. That slogan was never directed specifically at you."

Laying there in bed, cuddling, she sighed and turned to face him. "Why didn't we talk about this when we were kids?"

They had been so young, and both had been so afraid to face their feelings for one another.

"Because, being young and stupid, we lacked the confidence or the maturity to speak about things which troubled us back then. All we could do was ride the hype in school and hope we didn't come crashing down, looking like a fool."

A chuckle came from the darkness. "That's true. If you had won, I would have been so embarrassed."

"And when they declared you the winner, *I* was embarrassed. Looking back, the whole event seems so silly, and yet we let a childhood experience make us opponents for years."

If they had not been enemies, would they have gotten together sooner?

"Another sign of not being mature adults."

Her hand reached up, and she stroked his cheek. "When this is over, are we going to be friends now? Or go back to being enemies?"

What could he say?

As much as he wanted to be friends, he also wanted to be lovers, but he was frightened to let her close.

Would she be angry when she learned he's been using her to obtain his uncle's money?

Would she hate him?

"For fifteen years we've been enemies, I think I'd like to see what being friends is like," he said, as she rubbed her butt against his shaft, and he groaned. "Oh hell, Caitlyn, you're driving me crazy."

"What?"

Grabbing her hand, he placed it on his rock-hard penis. "Don't you know what you do to me?"

With a gasp, she pressed herself against him.

Was that her signal telling him she wanted him the same way he ached for her?

His lips found hers, and his mouth moved over her, taking possession, expressing his need, letting her know how much he wanted her. What he couldn't say with words, he showed her with his mouth. Her arms reached up and pulled him in tighter, and he groaned again.

She pushed his t-shirt away, her hands skimming down his body. The urge to rip her nightgown out of the way had him grabbing the material and tearing it away from her body. Hell, he would buy her a dozen new gowns, but he needed to touch her flesh immediately.

"Nathan," she moaned his name, his hands reaching for her breasts.

Twisting her nipples, he released her lips, and moved his mouth down to her tasty orbs.

Taking the pebbled kernel in his mouth, he tasted her, marveling at the silkiness of her.

A rapid knock at their bedroom door, caused them both to freeze.

What the hell?

"Caitlyn, hurry! They've just taken your father to the hospital by ambulance," her mother cried out.

Rolling onto his back, he sighed deeply, knowing the moment had been ruined.

Caitlyn jumped out of bed, and while he hated hospitals, he couldn't let her go alone.

What if the man died?

What if she needed him?

Standing, he searched for his pants. Soon they were dressed and met her mother in the living room, where she paced as she waited for them.

"I'll drive," he said, wondering when the family drama would end, but hoping and praying Mr. Beckett didn't die of a heart attack. Nathan had lost his own father that way, and he wouldn't wish the pain of that on anyone.

CHAPTER TWENTY-FOUR

*W*hen Caitlyn, Nathan and Louise walked into the emergency room, they were met by Heather, Whitney and Aaron.

"How is he?" Louise asked as they rushed into the waiting room. The cold sterile environment sent a shiver down Caitlyn's spine.

How many germs resided in the chairs, the tables, even the magazines?

"Nothing yet," Whitney said. "They're still examining him."

A sigh escaped Caitlyn as she stood with her sisters, shaking her head. During the best foreplay she'd ever had, her mother had knocked on their door. Another five minutes, and he would have been deep inside her, and she would have been experiencing the greatest sex of her life she could actually remember.

Once again, her family drama interrupted her, and yet, her father's life could be in danger. Glancing at Nathan, she stared at him in wonder. Damn, but she'd wanted to experience love-making with her husband.

"There's something you should know," Heather said, staring at Caitlyn and Nathan.

"Heather Diane, keep your mouth shut," her mother said. "You are not at liberty to say anything. That's my business."

"Mother it's time to confess," Heather said.

Tilting her head, Caitlyn frowned.

What was her mother hiding?

What did she not want the rest of them to know?

Heather pulled her mother aside, and the two of them walked down the hall arguing.

What happened to the relatively peaceful family she thought she belonged to?

Why did it seem like all they did was fight lately?

Sometimes she didn't have a clue what they argued about.

Whitney shook her head and raised her brows. Aaron tried not to laugh and glanced away.

"Mrs. Beckett?" A young physician stood in front of the swinging doors separating the waiting room from the examination rooms.

Her mother came hurrying down the aisle. "How is he?"

"He's fine. His EKG is normal. We did an ultrasound of the heart, and everything appears to be working properly. When I asked about stress in his life, he told me the two of you are going through a difficult time."

"Yes, we're separated," she confirmed.

Calm as a cucumber, her mother acted as if their separation was a normal thing, and her husband having an episode with his heart was an everyday occurrence.

Was Caitlyn the only one who seemed to think this behavior was abnormal?

The doctor smiled. "Why don't you go back and talk to him, and if everything is all right, then I'll release him to go home. Someone must stay with him tonight. He's not to be alone."

Oh, great!

Was she going to end up with both of her parents staying with Nathan and her?

Not fair.

Louise turned and gazed at Heather and Whitney. "Caitlyn has me. So one of you will need to sleep over at your father's."

Turning on her heel, her mother followed the doctor down the hall. Out of hearing, the girls all stared at one another.

"What are we going to do about this? It can't continue," Heather said.

"I'm still on my honeymoon," Whitney said.

"Hey, what about me?" Caitlyn replied. "I have Mother, and this is my honeymoon too."

"And you're doing a fine job with her," Heather said, smiling.

A laugh escaped Whitney.

The next two weeks were going to be crucial. This craziness needed to end and *now*.

"The better question, is how are we going to get them back together? That would solve all our problems," Whitney replied. "Our father is a cantankerous old coot, but they've been married a long time."

Maybe her parents *should* divorce. Obviously, her mother was not happy. Her father was a pain the ass to live with, so much so, once you left the house, you would rather sleep on the streets than return home.

A trickle of unease spiraled through Caitlyn as she stared at Heather.

Could her parents be arguing about her and Nathan?

But why?

They didn't pay any money on her wedding, or anything else for that matter.

"What were you trying to tell us Mother refused to let you speak about?"

"Can't say. It will come out soon enough." With a sigh, she shook her head. "All right, I'll take Daddy tonight, and tomorrow

I'll do my best to convince him to be more lenient towards Mother. I'll work on him. But I'm about to go into hibernation. No phone calls, no family drama, nothing, until I pass the bar exam. Do you all understand?"

"Yes," they all said in unison. "We'll only call you if someone is shot and killed," Caitlyn said. "And believe me, that could happen anytime."

Just then, her mother appeared, walking down the hall and smiling. "The doctor is going to release him and send him home."

"Did you kiss and make up?" Whitney asked.

"No, dear, not happening," she said. "In fact, I told him on Monday I would be contacting an attorney and filing for divorce."

What the hell!

The man is in the freaking *hospital*, and she tells him she's ending their marriage?

She glanced at Nathan for support, and he squeezed her hand. Then he mouthed the word "crazy."

Nodding her head, she agreed with him.

Exhausted, both emotionally and physically, Caitlyn let Nathan lead her out of the hospital. Humming to herself, like tonight was just another day in her grand scheme of things, her mother followed dutifully behind.

If Caitlyn ever had children, she must remember how her family acts, so as not to make the same mistakes.

After the trip to the emergency room, Nathan and Caitlyn cancelled their plans to go to Dallas. Until this family drama ended, she should stay close. Though her trip to St. Tropez was only days away. If her mother was still with them then, Caitlyn was planning to tell her she needed to go to Whitney's.

Saturday evening, Caitlyn observed her mother scurrying around. "Come on, you two, I'm taking you out to dinner."

Caitlyn came down after changing, and her mother glanced at her. "Oh, honey, I know you own something nicer you can wear. We're going to the most expensive restaurant in town. We're dressing up and celebrating tonight. Nathan, that suit you wore to Whitney and Aaron's wedding looked very nice on you."

Together, Nathan and Caitlyn trudged back up the stairs to change.

"Something's up."

"You're right," he said.

As they changed, she couldn't help but watch as he put on a crisp white linen shirt, and added a tie which matched her dress.

"Wow! You look handsome," she said. "And I love that your tie matches my dress."

A grin spread across his face, and he knelt to help her slide into some heels. "Whatever happens tonight, let's just go with the flow."

For the last month, they kissed and touched each other a lot more, and she liked the way his strong hands gripped her. The feel of his mouth against hers. In only a few days she would be leaving. Ninety-one days would soon be here, and it was hard to believe this was almost over.

And she wasn't ready for their marriage to end.

Releasing her, he walked across to his dresser and pulled out a gorgeous piece of jewelry. Seeing the size of the diamonds, she gasped.

"That dress is begging for you to wear this tonight. This necklace belonged to my mother."

"Are you sure?"

"Positive," he said, then clasped the diamonds around her neck.

Turning, she gazed in the mirror and smiled. "The necklace is beautiful."

His hands slid down her formfitting dress. "My wife is gorgeous. Every man in the restaurant is going to shoot daggers of envy at me. They're going to think I'm a lucky guy."

With a smile, she took his hand. Together they walked out of the bedroom and down the hall to the stairs. Since being forced to share his room, their relationship had changed. Instead of waiting out the days, she now looked forward to him coming home from work. The time they spent with each other, she enjoyed, especially the nights.

Terror filled her at the thought he was slowly winning her over. That her enemy was no longer the man she hated, but rather the man she was falling in love with.

Walking down the stairs, her mother took their picture. "Since I didn't get wedding photos, this will be a good substitute. Oh, Caitlyn, you would have made a beautiful bride!"

If she went to St. Tropez and found her a husband, they would pay their own ceremony, and not her family, not even her dress would be paid by them.

Suddenly, she realized something…the trip she had dreamed of for so long, no longer seemed quite as important.

Yet, everything depended on her taking that trip. *Everything*!

Once Nathan helped them both into the car and backed out of the driveway, he asked, "Where are we going?"

"The Cupid Hotel."

A zing spiraled through Caitlyn, and she glanced at Nathan. The hotel was where they'd held her sister's bachelorette party, and it was the only place in town which had a room big enough to hold a reception.

Oh my God!

Her mother was throwing them a wedding reception!

Suddenly, it dawned on her the reason her parents were fighting. Knowing her father, he didn't want to pay for this event, and her mother had insisted.

While she knew his lack of support shouldn't matter, it did. It hurt he would think so little of her marriage he refused to hold them a reception. However, her marriage would be ending as soon as they could get a divorce.

The union would be over, and her father could now throw *that* in her face.

How he paid for a party for a wedding which ended only a few days later.

Well, she would party like a rock star tonight and enjoy the fact her mother, at least, believed in her marriage. Reaching over, she squeezed Nathan's leg, and he glanced at her and nodded.

When had they developed this silent communication?

The man recognized what was going on only from the glance she'd given him.

Warmth spread through her, and though their union would soon end, tonight, she wanted to party with Nathan. They would celebrate with their family and friends the wedding which was never supposed to have been.

They pulled into the parking lot, and she glanced around. The lot was full of cars. After Nathan parked his own car, he walked around and opened her door, and then her mother's.

"Come on, ladies," he said, offering them each an arm as they strolled towards the hotel.

Once inside, her mother smiled, and Nathan held the door.

"*Surprise!*" a chorus of voices rang out.

A big banner hung in the front of the room.

Congratulations, Nathan and Caitlyn!

"Mom," Caitlyn said, as tears sprang to her eyes and the emotions in her throat threatening to choke her, "you didn't have to do this."

Her mother hugged her, and said, "Yes, I did. Your wedding was unconventional, sure, but we still needed to celebrate your vows. Weddings don't happen very often."

Guilt gripped Caitlyn and even more tears filled her eyes. For a moment, she wanted to confess, but Nathan took her by the hand and pulled her through the line of people, all there to congratulate the couple and wish them the best.

She felt like a fraud.

SYLVIA MCDANIEL

Her sisters, Aaron–*and even her father*!–waited at the end of the line.

"Consider this a real wedding reception," her mother said. "At the main table will be you and Nathan, along with your sisters and Aaron.

Music begin to play, and a DJ announced, "Please observe the happy couple's first dance together!"

Taking her by the hand, Caitlyn's husband led her out onto the floor, and they danced to a slow waltz.

"What are we going to do?"

In his embrace, he gazed down at her. "We're going to celebrate our marriage and party with our friends."

"But it's a lie," she said, gazing up into his emerald eyes. "Our marriage is about to end."

"Not tonight. Tonight, is our wedding night," he said, staring into her eyes.

Warmth cascaded through her.

"Stop thinking so much and enjoy the celebration your mother put together for us."

At the end of the song, his lips covered hers, and he kissed her until she feared her clothes were going to melt right off. Oh, how she wanted the world to recede and it just be her and Nathan.

Everyone cheered, and she turned to see her sisters wiping tears from their eyes. As she walked off, her father came towards her.

"My turn," he said, then took her onto the dance floor, where they performed the father-daughter dance.

Caitlyn looked over and saw her mother dancing with Nathan and smiled when she saw they were laughing and talking together.

"Is this party what you and Mother were fighting about?"

A grimace crossed his face. "Yes."

"All righty," she said. "Well, thank you, Daddy, for the reception. I know you don't like to spend any money on your daughters, but I didn't ask for this. And you didn't have to pay for my wedding."

The urge to flee from the floor was strong, but her mother had put in so much effort and had sacrificed nearly everything, so she didn't want to ruin this party for her.

The man she called Daddy–who she loved and hated, all at the same time–tensed in her arms. He cleared his throat and said, "When I was a kid, we didn't have enough food to eat. Taking care of you girls and your mother, I worried for years I wouldn't be able to support you. I'd made a vow my children would never go hungry."

"We never went hungry. But how much money do you need, before that little boy inside you is safe and secure?"

Stunned, he stared at her.

"It's not Mother or us girls you're trying to protect, but that little boy who had to do without food. Or are you willing to lose your family just so you can continue to be a miser?"

The song ended, and they parted ways. Immediately, Nathan came to her side, took her hand in his and brought it to his lips.

"Are you all right?"

"I'm fine," she lied. "I'm not the one with the problem, my father is."

Soon, everyone was up dancing on the floor, laughing and having a good time, until the food arrived.

Next the toasts begin. Some made her laugh, and some made her cry, but all she could think during the entire evening was this was all a farce. She'd lied to her family and friends just to achieve her goal of marrying a rich man, a means in order to take that trip to St. Tropez to find Mr. Perfect.

What made her any different from her father?

Who was she to judge him?

A cringe skirted along her spine when her father took the microphone to make a toast.

Oh dear, why did she have such a bad feeling about this?

"Nathan, you stole my little girl in Vegas. From the time you were twelve, you two have hated each other. I never really understood what all the drama was about, but you have clashed and fought all these years since this, until Vegas. The same night Whitney and Aaron were married, you two sucked down your liquor and woke up married. No one was more shocked than her mother and I to discover you and our daughter were husband and wife."

He paused and took a deep breath.

"To be honest, I never thought this marriage would last, and that's why I've been trying to get my wife to hold off on throwing such a grand party. Watching you tonight though, Nathan, I noticed you protect my little girl. I've seen the way you gaze at her, and frankly, I'm glad you're the man she married."

The crowd murmured in agreement, and a trickle of warmth spread through Caitlyn.

Really?

Did Nathan really look at her as her father described?

Sure, she felt his eyes on her, but they weren't supposed to fall in love. They were only supposed to be together for ninety-one days!

"While you grew up hating each other, I'm so glad you guys are now happily married. May you give your mother and me many grandkids and spend the rest of your days together, laughing and having fun."

Leaning into her husband, tears welling up in her eyes once more, but this time from the amazing toast from her father, Caitlyn whispered, "Oh no, Nathan, what are we going to do?"

He kissed her solidly on the mouth, and suddenly, her fears, her disappointments...*everything* melted away.

"Now, I have one more piece of business," her father said. "Louise will you come up here?"

Oh no, what was her father doing?

Most people in the audience didn't know they were separated. Most people didn't know they were fighting, and yet, he was bringing her mother right on up in front of everyone!

"Yes, dear," she said with a smile.

Caitlyn recognized that look. It was the "you better do good, or you are going to be severely punished for embarrassing me" smile.

With a nervous laugh, he gazed at her mother. "We've been married for almost thirty years. After that long, a man forgets how to court his wife, which you recently brought to my attention."

His hands shook.

"You and our daughters call me a miser. And you're all right; I am. Tonight, Caitlyn reminded me how smart she is, and I know I need to be more trusting in her judgement. At this stage in life, I'm always going to be tight with my money, but maybe I need to enjoy life a little more. This afternoon, while you and the girls were setting up for the party, I did a little shopping."

Dropping down to one knee, he smiled up at her and pulled out a small box from his pocket. Opening the jewelry box, he said, "Marry me once again, Louise. Marry me, and let's go on that vacation you've been dreaming about. Here are two airplane tickets to Italy."

Louise gasped and pulled him up to his feet. "You old fool! You know I love you more than anything. I'll marry you again—anytime, anyplace. From now on, when I say I want something, I need you to understand and help me obtain whatever that need may be, within reason of course. I love you, Milton, and I can't wait to go on this trip with you."

Everyone was crying now, and Whitney and Heather hugged each other. Tears streamed down Caitlyn's cheeks. "Oh thank God, they're going to be all right."

With a smile, Nathan pulled her close. "Somehow, I don't think your mother will be coming home with us tonight."

After that, they all danced the night away, clear up until

SYLVIA MCDANIEL

midnight, when everyone finally lined up outside and threw
birdseed at Nathan and Caitlyn as they made a mad dash to their
car.

Caitlyn turned to glance at Nathan as he pulled her through
the shower of seed. "Let's go home."

No matter what happened after tonight, at this moment, she
needed her husband.

CHAPTER TWENTY-FIVE

*T*he drive home was quiet and filled with tension—sexual tension.

Nathan kept glancing over at her and finally she reached out and placed her hand on his thigh.

"Hurry," she urged.

Those words had him almost flooring the car as they sped down Main Street towards his home. Once they pulled into the garage, she didn't wait for him to come around and open the door, but instead, met him at the back door.

Inside the house, she grabbed him and pulled her to him. This was the Caitlyn he remembered from their wedding night. Their lips melded together, and he moved her towards the stairs. Tonight, he wanted nothing to come between them.

Tonight, he wanted to show her with his body how much he cared about her. When they reached the bottom rung of the stairs, he broke the kiss and grabbed her hand.

Together, they raced up the stairs. At the bedroom door, he paused and glanced at her. "Tonight was so much fun."

"Yes," she said. "Let's continue the tradition and make tonight our honeymoon."

Her words surprised him, but they also filled him with warmth. If given the chance, he would like to make every night their honeymoon."

"Nathan," she groaned against his lips.

After the kiss, he moved his mouth next to her ear as he nuzzled her neck and earlobe, his tongue sliding across her skin. A shudder oscillated through her, and he smiled, knowing he affected her as much as she did him.

Standing in the doorway, gazing at him, her eyes were wide with expectation and desire, and anticipating what was about to happen. Like a caged lion, he freed the hunger raging through him for her.

"Caitlyn!" he gasped.

This woman, who had managed to wedge her way into his heart almost from the first day of elementary school, met his gaze head on, her breathing quick and shallow. Pushing her against the door, his body covered hers, pressing into her soft volup-tuous curves, his rock-solid erection snug against her womanly mound. His mouth came down hard on her full lips, expressing his need.

A moan rent the air, deep in her throat, and he relished the sound. While he caressed her luscious mouth, his hands slid down her dress, needing to touch her satiny flesh.

Abruptly, she broke the seal of their mouths. "I want to feel you," she demanded.

"Yes," he whispered, barely able to talk, his need for her so great.

Her fingers unbuttoned his shirt as they trailed from his neck to his waist, where she undid the button on his dress pants. In a matter of seconds, she had stripped him bare where he stood before her, his penis jutting out proudly.

"Your turn," he said, as he unzipped her dress, then slid the garment down to the floor. With a snap, he unhooked her bra, her gorgeous breasts spilling out, tempting him to stop undressing her and get to work on sucking those luscious orbs of hers, but he wanted her as naked as he'd seen her when she'd done the Cupid Stupid Dance.

He peeled the strip of underwear from her, and she kicked off her heels.

Now they were both nude, standing in front of the door, their breaths constricted, lost in the building heat between them.

Simultaneously, they swayed toward each other, reaching out at the same time, as he dragged her mouth to his, wanting to consume her lips. A moan floated through the room, and he was shocked to realize the sound had come from him as he crushed her lips beneath his own, longing guiding him.

Breaking their kiss, he leaned his forehead against hers. "I've wanted you long before our wedding. Now I don't want to give you up."

"Shh..." she said. "Concentrate on now, not tomorrow."

So he did.

A small boy in kindergarten could not have fallen in love with a young girl, but it seemed whenever he thought of a girl in school, it was always Caitlyn who came to mind. Yet they had been enemies for so very long. Too long.

"Do you have a condom?" she asked, her voice soothing, her breath whispery.

"Yes," he groaned.

A shiver rippled through her.

"Are you cold? Let me warm you." Pulling her down with him to the bed, desire flowed through his veins like a flash flood in the rain forest.

"Not cold. Hot with need for you," she panted, her fingertips running down his chest, his stomach, and ending at his manhood.

As she wrapped her hand around him, he groaned, the sound

echoing in the room. Full to bursting with urgency for her as she massaged him, until his blood throbbed with enough heat to melt ice caps.

"Caitlyn," he whispered, as he gripped her head, holding her mouth hostage. His fingers tangled in her hair, not letting her escape his kiss.

His hands slid down her neck to her shoulders as he teased her, until he reached her chest. Cupping her pale globes, he released her lips and bent to lift the weight of one breast to his mouth eager, to taste her.

Why was Caitlyn different from any other woman?

From their childhood to their wedding night in Vegas, everything about her was unique.

Gently, he pulled on her nipple, sucking as much of her into his mouth as he could as she bucked wildly against him, her moans loud in the bedroom. As her hands moved to his head, trapping him against her breasts, trying to give him more access to her body, her breath became more ragged and harsher.

What had started as just a way for him to obtain the funds his uncle had left him, had now turned his world upside down and changed him. He didn't want her to leave, but to stay and explore this craving which existed between them.

But she didn't believe he was a billionaire.

With a gentle stroke, he glided his hand down her body, skimming over her flat abdomen, then continuing down until his caress touched her intimate folds.

"Nathan," she whimpered.

There was so much passion flowing between them, he feared he would not last.

"Your skin is like satin," he said, as he delved inside her center. Slowly, he stroked her, watching her face change. The quilt was gripped tightly in her fists, as his fingers teased her until she squirmed and moaned.

Tightening around him, she screamed, shuddering, as her

passion-filled eyes stared straight into his soul. Emotion swelled within him as his chest shattered with love and shaking him to his core.

Their wedding night had been fun, but tonight, the joining was filled with emotion and lust, and the need to remain together.

But would she stay?

For him, and not for his money?

Not ready to analyze his emotions, he quickly reached into the nightstand and pulled out a condom. With a rip, he opened the package and sheathed himself with the rubber, then parted her legs with his.

They fit perfectly together, her breasts against his chest, her hips supporting him, his shaft nestled between the juncture of her thighs, right where he belonged. Unable to hold back any longer, he entered her in a single swift movement.

"Oh, Nathan!" she murmured.

Helpless to look away, he stared into her eyes, and believed they were joined as one as he moved inside her, stroking her, loving her, as they rode the waves of passion together. Holding onto one another, she clutched his back, clinging to him, and he wanted it no other way.

They were enemies, they were lovers, and yet never had he experienced such lovemaking as what he felt within her arms. A compressing spiral of need consumed him, and as much as he wished he could last longer, he couldn't.

With a guttural cry, he slammed into her body, his body convulsing with his release.

No matter what happened in their future, he would always remember tonight. For tonight, his enemy had tamed him and made her his. Tonight, she had captured his heart, and he admitted to himself he didn't want their marriage to end.

He wanted Caitlyn as his wife forever…but what was he going to do?

Satiated, he rolled them to their sides, tucking her tightly against his body, his heart pounding, his pulse racing. When she glanced up at him, he saw her eyes were half-lidded, spent from their intimacy, and he reached down and kissed her on the lips.

Could he convince her not to end their marriage?

CHAPTER TWENTY-SIX

*W*hat had she done?

Nathan lay naked curled around her, sleeping, while she stared into the darkness. The travel documents were ready. The trip was paid for with a short-term loan.

If she backed out of the deal with Nathan, she would lose her business.

What if this was still just a temporary arrangement for him?

A business deal which meant nothing?

No, she made a vow to herself, she risked everything to go St. Tropez. She would not let her feelings for Nathan sway her. No matter what, she would take her vacation and find a rich man to marry her.

With a sigh, she wiped away a tear.

How had she fallen in love with this man?

Somehow, the enemy had conquered and tamed her, and she belonged only to him. And that's what frightened her so terribly much!

Regardless of whether he wanted her, she would go to St. Tropez. When she'd made the travel arrangements, she'd thought it would be best if she left right after she received the money.

Now she had no choice.

While she was gone, the firestorm over their break-up and impending divorce would ease, but now she wondered if she was truly crazy.

How could she enjoy St Tropez with a broken heart?

She had only two options: Stay here and risk being humiliated, broke and lonely; or follow through with her plans and carry on with a shattered heart.

Turning over, she gazed at him in the darkness. What a mess she found herself in, yet, she'd never been happier. Looking back, these weeks with Nathan were the happiest she'd ever had, even with her family creating so much drama.

Sometime during the last eighty-nine days, she had fallen in love with him.

With so little time left, what could she do now?

Fear caused her heart to spike, her blood rushing through her like she was being chased.

Somehow, she needed to go now. She needed to leave tomorrow. If she waited until day ninety-one, she would never go. Her dreams of marrying a rich man would never be fulfilled.

But why did it now seem as though her plan was no longer important, when it had once been the only thing which mattered to her?

But if she left, he didn't have to pay her. Without the cash, she would lose everything.

No matter what, she would continue on her path. She would go to St. Tropez, find a wealthy husband, and somehow–maybe?– her heart would heal.

How could she give her heart away to another man, when one man had already claimed her soul?

CHAPTER TWENTY-SEVEN

*T*he next morning, they woke to day ninety. Only one more night together unless he asked her to stay.

"Good morning," he said.

"Good morning."

Dark circles shadowed her eyes as if she'd gotten little slept. An air of dejectedness hung about her, and he wondered if making love until the wee hours of the morning had drained her too much.

"You okay?"

"Just tired," she said. "That was quite the party."

A smile crossed his face. "Yes, it was!" He placed his hand on her thigh and cleared his throat, before saying, "Look, I know it's Sunday, but I've got to run into the office. We're having a conference call regarding Aaron's development, and this was the only day we could meet. I'll be home as soon as I can."

They had so much to talk about. His chest ached with the need to confess his love and ask her to stay. No way did he want to let her go.

But right now, he had to get going. Though he longed to just stay with her all day.

With his pending appointment looming, he jumped out of bed, anxious to get it done and get back to her.

This morning, he felt as if he could conquer the world. Last night, the party had made him realize how much he didn't want this marriage to end. How much he wanted Caitlyn as his wife forever.

Last night, he'd realized he loved her.

Quickly, he showered, then grabbed a bite to eat and was soon ready to leave. Before he did, he ran back upstairs to tell her he was leaving.

He found her still lying in bed, curled in a ball.

When he walked over to her, he leaned down and gave her a gentle kiss. "Why don't you rest? Tonight, we should talk."

A weak grin spread across her face, and she nodded.

Reaching up, she pulled his lips down to hers and kissed him thoroughly. It was a deep kiss, one that made him want to crawl back in bed with her. When they released, she stared up at him.

"Our time is almost over," she whispered.

"Tonight, we're going to make some decisions."

"Bye, Nathan," she said with a sad smile.

A twinge spiraled through him.

"See you *later*," he said, and though he didn't want to leave, he knew he had to attend this meeting.

As he rushed out the door, he already wished he were rushing back in.

CHAPTER TWENTY-EIGHT

*A*s soon as Nathan left, Caitlyn jumped out of bed and hurried to the closet to grab her suitcases.

She couldn't stay any longer. She couldn't wait until tomorrow.

If she didn't go now, she would never leave. If she didn't go now, her dreams of marrying a rich man would be forever dashed.

Because she loved Nathan, and she was certain he didn't feel the same.

She was so sure the talk he mentioned was one where he planned to remind her of their agreement.

Her flight left tomorrow night, but she still had to drive to Dallas. Tomorrow, she could spend the day shopping...or moping in her hotel room alone.

Quickly she showered and packed her bags.

As she walked through the house one last time, sadness filled her eyes with tears. So much had happened in this house, that now the Victorian felt like *her* home. It was here she'd fallen in love with Nathan. It was here she'd given him her heart.

Sitting down at the kitchen table, she wrote him a note. Yes, she knew she should call her mother or her sisters, but she feared they would try to talk her out of fulfilling her dream, and there would be so much to explain, so she didn't.

The dream was quickly slipping away from her, and if she didn't leave now, Mr. Perfect would be gone for good...or at least, any small drop of desire she had left to do this would be gone for good.

No matter what, she had to go now, or she would be lost.

With a final glance at the home she'd grown to love, almost as much as she loved the man who lived there, she strolled out the door, got into her car, and headed towards Dallas.

Towards her future.

Towards her rich husband.

Even as her heart shattered.

Was she crazy?

Maybe Nathan was planning to ask her to stay?

But she couldn't take that chance. Because if he didn't ask her to remain his wife, she couldn't let him see her break in front of him.

CHAPTER TWENTY-NINE

*S*ometimes she just doubled down on the crazy. As she lay on the beautiful beach of St. Tropez and gazed at all the sexy men in speedo's, thongs and other types of beachwear, she realized she didn't want a single one of them. They could be the richest man on earth, and frankly, she wasn't interested.

Staring at the water, tears welled up in her eyes, as they had so many times since leaving Cupid, but this time, she gave in and allowed herself to cry.

Gorgeous white sand, hunky men and sadness all combined to overwhelmed her.

What in the hell had she done!

Life gave her exactly what she wanted, yet a billionaire no longer held any appeal. The memory of her conversation the night of the party with her father rattled her.

Was she like him in that she searched for money to satisfy the little girl who had always been told no?

Growing up, her life had been typical, but she'd always wanted something the other children had and could remember constantly being told no.

For Christmas one year, she'd only asked for one thing: a speedster bike.

Instead, she'd received the parts to make her old bike look as much like a speedster, that the old rusted bucket of metal could.

Clearly, it wasn't the same.

All the girls in junior high had worn beautiful, formfitting boots. Hers, however, were the cheaper brand, which looked much like plastic, and flopped around her skinny legs.

Always it seemed she'd had to beg for what she wanted, and always she was given something less. Yet, she never did go hungry, so there was that.

Was her search for a billionaire the result of her own childhood?

Was she trying to satisfy that little girl, like her father still tried to complete the little boy inside himself?

The memory of Nathan dancing with her at the party and the kiss they exchanged at the end, made her sad.

Oh, how she would give anything to be with him right this moment!

A handsome man stopped beside her chair and smiled down at her. "You need some sunscreen rubbed on your beautiful skin?"

The urge to tell him to screw off was strong, but he'd done nothing wrong to deserve it. *She* had.

"Thank you, but no," she said, quickly sending him on his way.

This vacation had cost her nearly thirty thousand dollars, and all she would go home with was a tan and a broken heart.

In fact, she wondered why she continued to lay here on this beach, when she could be on the next flight home.

The only reason she even came here was to fulfill her promise to herself that she would take a fabulous vacation, and while there, she'd meet and marry a rich man.

But this beautiful island didn't feel right. It felt all wrong. Like she didn't belong.

Suddenly, she flew to her feet.

She *was* crazy!

Cupid-crazy-in-love with a man who had once been her enemy, and she was going to go home, back to *him*. If he would take her back, she would do whatever it took to make him happy.

Coming here had been a huge mistake. A terrible blunder. Leaving Nathan, she realized she loved him and only him. If he would take her back, she would be satisfied to be as poor as church mice if it ever came to that.

Money no longer mattered. Love did, and she loved Nathan.

CHAPTER THIRTY

*a*aron stared at him. "What the hell is the matter with you?"

Nathan glanced at his best friend.

What could he say?

That the woman he loved left him to go to St. Tropez to meet and marry a billionaire?

That obviously he had not been enough for her?

"Whitney's really worried about Caitlyn. She's left multiple messages, but she hasn't called her back. She and Heather met for lunch today. Be prepared for the Beckett women to come crashing on your doorstep tonight."

Great, just great! That's all he needed. These sisters were crazy, and Caitlyn was even crazier.

"I'm going to tell you a secret. You're being sworn to secrecy, though I'm sure it will all come out in a few weeks anyway."

He spent the next thirty minutes telling Aaron the truth behind his and Caitlyn's marriage, and how on Sunday evening, he'd come home to find Caitlyn long gone. All she'd left was a note saying she couldn't stay a moment longer.

Shaking his head, Aaron stared at him. "So she's in St. Tropez, searching for a rich husband?"

"Yes, and what she doesn't know, is the reason I did this, was so I could inherit my uncle's billions."

Funny how they had both been working towards something and had each received exactly what they wanted, only to learn it wasn't what *he* wanted any longer.

He no longer cared about the money. All he wanted–all he *needed*–was Caitlyn.

"Do you love her?"

"Since elementary school, I've had a crush on her. In junior high, I screwed up terribly, and setting her up to marry me was wrong. But I'm the one this all backfired on. I'm the one who fell in love with her."

Aaron nodded. "If you love her, why aren't you fighting for her? Why haven't you gone after her? If that was Whitney, I'd follow her, not giving her a moments rest, persuading her I'm the only man for her."

But he wasn't who she wanted. And yet, the other night, she'd called his name out in passion, and when he'd left the next morning, he'd felt certain she loved him.

A frown crossed his face. "I want her to love me for me, not for my money, or because I'm her last chance."

"Have you told her you love her?"

"No," he admitted, wishing he had whispered the words their last night together, or even the following morning.

" Then maybe she doesn't think you want her. What if she thought you were going to break things off with her on the ninety-first day and took off to avoid that, because it was going to hurt her too much?"

Nathan sat there for a moment thinking over what Aaron had said. They'd never confessed their feelings; they'd only ever expressed their growing emotion using their bodies.

Why hadn't he told her he was falling in love with her?

"Get on the next plane and go after her, unless you're okay with another man taking what's yours," Aaron said. "Fight for what you want."

Nathan stood and clasped his friend around the back giving him a hug. "Damn, that makes sense! Instead of fighting for what I want, like a fool, I sat here feeling sorry for myself. Boss, I'm going to be gone for a while. I'll be in St. Tropez!"

When he stepped back, Aaron shook his head. "What do you want me to tell her sisters and her mother? Because I'm telling you, there will be no peace until they learn what is going on."

"Tell them we're on our honeymoon in St. Tropez. And do not disturb us!"

A grin spread across Aaron's face. "Good luck, man!"

CHAPTER THIRTY-ONE

$\mathscr{C}$aitlyn was relieved to be going home. St Tropez was beautiful, luxurious, and everything a dream vacation should have been, except her heart was back in Cupid, Texas, and she needed to get home.

Like a coward, she had run from her feelings, and now she had to see if she could salvage her love and her marriage.

As she exited the car, she paid the cab driver and headed into the airport.

Time to go home.

Standing in line at the ticket counter, she thought she saw Nathan. She closed her eyes and opened them again, and shock flooded her.

It *was* him!

"Nathan!" she called.

What the hell was he doing here?

Her heart began to pound in her chest, and she all but ran to him, dragging her luggage behind her, until they began to flip and twist, so she released them, leaving them behind, and continued running.

"Caitlyn!" He rushed to her side. "Why aren't you at the hotel?"

People scurried around them to make their flights in time, but she couldn't wait any longer. She had to tell him now. Grabbing onto his arms, as if she feared he would run away, a tear slipped down her cheek.

"This is not where I belong. I'm a married woman. When I dreamed of coming here, I was single, looking for something I believed I needed to be happy. But you've shown me, I don't need a billionaire. I love you, Nathan."

A smile spread across his face. "I came here to fight for the woman I love. You're my wife, I love you, and I don't want any billionaire other than myself stealing you away from me."

Wait.

What did he just say?

"You *love* me?"

"More than you will ever know. I've loved you since elementary school. We were meant to be together."

She released a sob of happiness and relief, then fell into his arms. "Forgive me. Sometimes I'm a crazy, stupid fool. I don't know why I risked everything to come here and find love, when it was back in Cupid all along."

His mouth came crashing down on hers, and he kissed her deeply. It felt as if she had come home, and she knew right there, in his embrace, was where she belonged.

When he released her, he smiled. "What if we do this...we can pretend we're strangers, and I'll be the billionaire you meet and fall in love with."

Filled with love, she laughed as they began walking arm in arm towards the entrance, grabbing all their luggage along the way. "I don't need a billionaire any longer."

"Is that right? Well, damn. I guess I'd better go back home then." He stopped and began to turn back.

She laughed and pulled his arm to get him turned back around.

"I'm over all that, Nathan. I love *you*. You're not a billionaire, and I'm okay with that."

"Actually, I am," he said. "Why do you think I needed you to marry me? My uncle's will stated I had to be married before I could inherit his billions."

Stunned, Caitlyn stopped in the middle of the airport, turned to face him, and stared at him. "You're a billionaire?"

"Yes, I am," he said with a grin.

She remained frozen in shock for several long moments, but then finally laughed and took his arm. "How ironic is this! But I'm telling you, it doesn't matter to me anymore. I would have loved you even if you were broke, and I'll love you if you lose every dime you have, and we end up being broke in the future. But...you know...try not to let that happen. Okay?" Her eyes sparkled as she teased him.

Laughing, he pulled her to him and kissed her on the lips again.

Suddenly, she pulled away. "Hey! You know what, Nathan? Maybe there *is* some truth to that superstition. We're together, aren't we? We need to tell Heather the Cupid Stupid Dance works!"

"Not now, my crazy wife. We're officially on our honeymoon. No other crazy family members are allowed until we go home."

I LOVED this couple so much. They were so immature and they both had so much to learn. I hope you enjoyed them as much as I did. Turn the page for sneak peak at Cupid's Bachelorette.

"I want what you have," Dustin Torres told his best friend and boss, Aaron Johnson, in his expensive sleek office. "Since I sold my game to a major toy company, the royalties have paid me well. I'm now a billionaire, but I want a wife and family. I want happiness."

Dustin had been shocked at how well his video game sold after Aaron helped him find the right company to purchase it. And now he wanted the rest of what he thought a great life would require. A loving wife and family.

Pictures of Aaron's wife, Whitney, graced the credenza behind him including a wedding photo of her in her bridal gown, with such a beautiful expression of love that Dustin felt jealous.

All he wanted was a woman to gaze at him like Whitney did Aaron. With a sigh, he had made a life for himself now he wanted to share it with someone.

He'd called this meeting to tell Aaron of his plans to step down from his position at EJ Construction, which was Aaron's pet project. After he made his billions, he was building homes for the less fortunate in their hometown of Cupid, Texas.

"Congratulations on the royalties. No wonder you bought that fancy new sports car. I thought I was paying you too much."

Dustin grinned. "No, but it's time I stepped down and let someone else take over."

Aaron frowned. "Believe me, I've been in your shoes. You make the money, your business is successful and then women begin to hound you. It's why I moved to Cupid."

Women were not chasing Dustin and he was glad. He wanted someone who would love him for who he was and not his bank account. Only he knew the truth about his recent cash flow, and Aaron was the first person he shared the information with.

The thought of women hounding him was hilarious. He wasn't a bad looking guy, but he had always been the quieter, geekier kind of man who women didn't find appealing. Especially, beautiful society types.

There was no room for a geek with a society girl.

"Most people don't know I've made a billion dollars and I'd like to keep it that way. But I would like to spend more time finding someone to spend my life with, working on another game, and maybe even some traveling. If I work for EJ Construction, my time is spent working with contractors. I've made the money, now I'd like to live a little."

Aaron leaned back in his chair and sighed. "I understand you want to quit. I get it. Now you want to pursue things that are important to you. That's why I'm here building houses for those less fortunate in our community. But right now, I need you. Is there any way you can stay on until after Whitney has the baby? She's due in two months. Her sister, Caitlyn, is due anytime. Lord help us if Heather gets pregnant. Their parents will go crazy with an explosion of grandbaby happiness."

Envy filled Dustin at the way the two women found love and were now fulfilling their dreams of having a family. It was what he wanted. Since his own family was scattered across the country, he felt lonely and missed them.

And his widowed mother had decided now was the time to date. She dated more than he ever had. After his father passed away, his mother moved into a retirement community where she appeared to be dating as many of the unmarried men as possible. Any day now, he expected a call that she had remarried and he had a stepfather.

But when was it Dustin's time to find love?

Gazing at Aaron, Dustin realized he couldn't abandon his best friend. Aaron had helped him find the right company to send his game to and encouraged him to keep trying when the rejections started to come in. Without him, he would not be where he was today.

There was no way he could walk away. Aaron asked him to come to work for him and help build the neighborhood that honored his dead mother. And for the last two years, Dustin had worked for Aaron. But now he felt the urge to go in search of his own happiness.

Now was his time to find the love of his life. And yet, he would have to wait at least four months. He could book a cruise and hope he would meet someone on a floating ship.

"All right. I'll even stay until the baby is two months old. That will give you some time to adjust to your new family life. But then I'm going in search of my own life. I want what you have. A nice home, a woman you love, and a family on the way."

Aaron grinned and leaned forward. "Then do what I did."

"What?"

"Dance naked around the Cupid statue."

That's right. That's how Aaron met Whitney. Dustin had forgotten.

"And get arrested?"

"Valentine's Day is coming up in two days. It's the perfect time. Whitney picked me up running naked down the street. She saved me from going to jail."

That was his biggest fear. The sheriff in town had put out warnings about doing the Cupid Dance on Valentine's Day. He cautioned, "Don't fall for the superstition. It's still against the law to be naked in a public place. Don't ruin your reputation." But then again, what kind of reputation did Dustin have?

A lonely gamer who worked hard and stayed home most nights. The only time he went out was when Nathan called him and they met for a drink. What could dancing around the statue hurt? He'd never believed in the superstition, but there were many people in town who claimed that's how they met their true love.

And now suddenly, he was considering doing the Cupid Dance. If it helped Aaron, why shouldn't he give it a try?

"Tell me what I need to do," he said, thinking he was completely crazy. But if it would get him what he wanted, doing that silly dance could be worth the risk.

Aaron laughed. "You go to the park right before midnight, you take your clothes off, and at the sound of the old clock chiming, you run around the statue three times chanting, 'Oh, Cupid, find me my true love.'"

"That's dorky," Dustin said. Even a geek like him thought it sounded silly.

His friend chuckled. "Yes, it is and you feel so stupid while you're running and saying the words, but I'm telling you it works."

No, there was no way that a dumb town superstition would find him the woman of his dreams. Not unless she resided in jail.

"I can see you're skeptical. I tell you what. If you meet a woman and she is your true love, then you work pro bono for me for the next four months. But if you don't meet anyone, then I'll pay you double and you can leave right after the baby is born."

Now that was a deal. He was showing that he didn't believe in this nonsense.

"If I meet a woman and we end up together, then I'll donate my salary to helping a needy family get into one of the new homes in our subdivision."

Aaron's face lit up. "That's a deal. But now you're committed and you have to do the Cupid Dance."

What had Dustin just agreed to?

"Yes, and if I end up in jail, you're going to bail me out."

"You do know that my sister-in-law, Heather, is now the assistant district attorney in town. And she handles these cases all the time."

"Oh, great," Dustin said, remembering Heather from the wedding. The woman was a beauty and he'd hate to have her prosecute him for being naked in a public place.

"You've got two nights to prepare before Cupid's arrow pierces your heart."

Wow, Aaron really did believe in this nonsense and his friend somehow managed to convince him that he should do the Cupid Dance. When it didn't work, he would book his cruise.

"I'm looking forward to leaving right after Whitney has the baby," he said with a grin, teasing his friend. Because when he met no one, then he could leave earlier.

Why in the world would a woman want to meet a running naked man? It seemed preposterous.

"Don't count on it, my friend. Let's go grab a drink. See if Nathan wants to join us. I've heard that once the baby arrives, you're both tied down."

The thought of his friend being a father made Dustin smile.

"Yes, but how exciting. A son or a daughter."

Aaron smiled. "I can't wait. Whitney is growing bigger and bigger, but she's beautiful, and soon we're going to be parents."

Dustin smiled, but inside he felt jealous. Aaron was a lucky man. A wife and family and someone to hold him at night. Everything that Dustin wanted.

Available at Your Favorite Retailer

PLEASE LEAVE A REVIEW

Did you enjoy the book? Reviews help authors. I would appreciate you posting a review.

Follow Sylvia on Facebook

Sign up for my new book alert at **www.SylviaMcDaniel.com** and receive a complimentary book.

Contemporary Romance
Burnett Brides Contemporary Times
Travis
Tanner
Tucker
Joshua
Jacob
Justin

Return to Cupid, Texas
Cupid Stupid
Cupid Scores
Cupid's Dance
Cupid Help Me!
Cupid Cures
**Cupid's Heart
Cupid Santa
**Cupid Second Chance
Cupid Charmer
Cupid Crazy
Cupid's Bachelorette
Cupid Games
Return to Cupid Box Set Books 1-3
Cupid Help Me Box Set Books 4-6
**The Unlucky Bride

Contemporary Romance
My Sister's Boyfriend
The Wanted Bride
The Reluctant Santa
The Relationship Coach
Secrets, Lies, & Online Dating

ALSO BY

Bride, Texas Multi-Author Series
**The Unlucky Bride

Lipstick and Lead 2.0
Nailing the Hit Man
Nailing the Billionaire
Nailing the Single Dad

Secrets of Mustang Island
Secrets of a Summer Place
Secrets of a Runaway Bride
Secrets From the Past

The Langley Legacy
Collin's Challenge

Short Sexy Reads
Racy Reunions Series
Paying For the Past
Her Christmas Lie
Cupid's Revenge

Western Historicals
A Hero's Heart
Second Chance Cowboy
Ethan

American Brides
**Katie: Bride of Virginia

Angel Creek Christmas Brides
Charity
Ginger
Minnie

Cora

The Burnett Brides Series
The Rancher Takes A Bride
The Outlaw Takes A Bride
The Marshal Takes A Bride
The Christmas Bride
Boxed Set

Lipstick and Lead Series
Desperate
Deadly
Dangerous
Daring
**Determined
Deceived
Defiant
Devious
Lipstick and Lead Box Set Books 1-4
**Quinlan's Quest

Mail Order Bride Tales
**A Brother's Betrayal
**Pearl
**Ace's Bride

Scandalous Suffragettes of the West
**Abigail
Bella
Mistletoe Scandal

Southern Historical Romance
A Scarlet Bride
Charity

The Cuvier Women
Wronged
Betrayed
Beguiled
Boxed Set

** Denotes a sweet book.

Want to learn about my new releases before anyone else? Sign up for my New Book Alert and receive a free book.

USA Today Best-selling author, Sylvia McDaniel obviously has too much time on her hands. With over eighty western historical and contemporary romance novels, she spends most days torturing her characters. Bad boys deserve punishment and even good girls get into trouble. Always looking for the next plot twist, she's known for her sweet, funny, family-oriented romances.

Married to her best friend for over twenty-five years, they recently moved to the state of Colorado where they like to hike, and enjoy the beauty of the forest behind their home with their spoiled dachshund Zeus. (He has his own column in her newsletter.)

Their grown son, still lives in Texas. An avid football watcher, she loves the Broncos and the Cowboys, especially when they're winning.

www.SylviaMcDaniel.com
Sylvia@SylviaMcDaniel.com
The End!

www.ingramcontent.com/pod-product-compliance
Lightning Source LLC
Chambersburg PA
CBHW071238170626
46809CB00015BA/2668